I0691413

Discipline

First Edition

Published by The Nazca Plains Corporation
Las Vegas, Nevada
2008

ISBN: 978-1-934625-07-1

Published by

The Nazca Plains Corporation ®
4640 Paradise Rd, Suite 141
Las Vegas NV 89109-8000

PUBLISHER'S NOTE
Discipline is a work of fiction created wholly by *Christopher Trevor's* imagination. All characters are fictional and any resemblance to any persons living or deceased is purely by accident. No portion of this book reflects any real person or events.

Cover, Russell Duparcq
Art Director, Blake Stephens

Dedication

For Pat, thanks for much inspiration and you are welcome for the tears...

Discipline

First Edition

Christopher Trevor

Contents

"Damn it! Get over here, boy! You're really gonna get it this time!"

What is it in hearing those words—or in uttering them!—that sends the male heart racing, the stomach plummeting, speeds the breathing, and, inevitably, sends a strange charge straight to the groin?

What's it going to be? A trip to the woodshed? A gym class paddling? A classroom caning? Or just an old-fashioned, over-the-knee spanking?

And will those pants be headed south?

Male/male discipline—at home, in school, at the fraternity, in the service, in prison—is so ancient and cross-cultural no one can be quite sure how it got started. Some who condemn it have referred to it as "symbolic sodomy", and that's probably a good enough explanation. After all, apes are known to expose their backsides to the dominant male in the community as a sign of submission, and somewhere in the distant veil of the past, some man discovered that a stiff swatting (rather than a deep plowing) might make a greater impression and provide a greater deterrent to the misbehavior of the human male.

The rump, of course, is uniquely designed for such punishment. "Those round, fleshy mounds upon which one sits," as the dictionary says, can absorb a thrashing that would leave any other part of the body bloody and broken. Just try to imagine taking that razor strop to a guy's shins! Too, frankly, a sore behind is not going to keep that boy from his chores in the fields the next day the way a flogging of the shoulders or back would.

But there is more to it than that. There is that heady mix of pain and humiliation—whether you administer it or are subjected to it. From an early age, boys are taught to be proud of their pricks, but embarrassed by their bottoms. Note sometime, in a crowded corridor, how differently men and women make way for someone while still protecting their most private parts. Women turn to face the wall—shielding their breasts and pussies. Men back against the wall so that most vulnerable of spots, that backdoor, is out of harm's way.

There is that strange male notion of contrition and punishment, of justice, of the purifying nature of suffering itself. "What does not kill me makes me stronger", the saying goes, though doubtless there's many the boy through the millennia at least for a short time just wished he were dead after a real raw hiding. There is, after discipline properly conducted, a real sense that the slate has been wiped clean, that the bad deed has been exorcised by fire, and the miscreant is cleansed. It's the notion of spanking as an act of love, of a traditional way to tame youthful high spirits or to settle scores without inflicting great bodily harm. The Book of Proverbs tells us that the man who does not punish his son does not love him, and, until very recent times, that seemed to be the common wisdom.

One final note—those who got their tails tanned over the centuries probably caught on to one other aspect of the whole procedure. The rear end—rooted just like the genitals in evolution's reptilian's cloacae—is richly endowed with nerves. That's why getting a whacking hurts so much. But, too, it also means that there comes a point where the brain wails, "Enough!", and opens the floodgates of our body's own drugs, our endorphins. You have to wonder sometimes if those really bad boys down the years had simply discovered Daddy Nature's fastest route to getting high.

So, kick back, enjoy yourself, and learn a thing or two about DISCIPLINE!

- Eddie Knapps-

Introduction

It was several years ago now. I was on a crowded subway train in the city of Boston heading to early morning class. Once again I was late for class. The train was packed with early morning commuters. The person next to me was somehow managing to drink a cup of coffee while holding on to the handrail above and reading a local personals newspaper. You have to realize this was years before online chat rooms or the internet. You would see very interesting and creative ads placed in the personals.

Now I know it's not good form to read someone else's newspaper but since the train was so crowded and we were practically joined at the hip I thought I'd make this one exception. The section of the paper facing me just happened to be "men for men". Perfect. Now remember this was years ago. My twenty something year old mind did not need much to get it going. Hell, my forty something year old mind does not need much to get it going. There was this one ad that jumped out at me. It was very simple.

Discipline: the ability to instruct a person to follow a code of conduct. To adhere to certain set ways, and certain behaviors. To find out more reply to this ad.

My mind was racing. That's all I needed to read. The thoughts occupied my mind throughout the remainder of the subway ride and well into my very busy day of classes. I often wondered what I would have found if I had answered the ad. Of course my imagination thought up several scenes that could have taken place, all of them sexual of course. Remember, I was in my early twenties. Did the person who placed the ad want to teach a young man about discipline? Was he a typical daddy type of person? Or perhaps it was someone who was looking for more control in his life. Perhaps an executive who gets tired of being in control all the time and secretly desires someone else taking over.

We've collected several stories that have some form of discipline attached to them. As you read through the stories think of that ad on the subway that I saw. Perhaps the same author has penned a story in this book.

-Ron Bossman-

For the Love of Mankind

Written by: Dutch Roberts

As Apollo burst from the dark, cool interior of the forest, radiant, warm rays of light did the same, from far above, piercing the dense, grey clouds that blanketed the sky. As he sprinted across the open field before him, the glowing beams struck his smooth, olive skin, causing the numerous droplets of dew, which speckled his lean torso, to glisten and sparkle.

"Oh, Artemis, how I do love the coming of spring!" he sang to his twin sister, who was nearly on his heels, matching not only his speed, but his every graceful move.

The two proceeded swiftly over the lush, emerald terrain, their bare feet hardly disturbing the moist, rich land below them.

"I know you do, dear brother, for it is the spring, as well as the coming summer, that you cherish the most," Artemis replied, with a look of affection on her normally stoic, yet radiant face. "That, as well as the stunning, scantily-clad specimens of man that seems to become far too abundant this time of the year."

"Beloved sister, you know me all too well," said Apollo, with a mischievous grin upon his full lips and a devilish gleam in his bright eyes.

"Far better than most," Artemis replied with an impish smile of her own. "And that is why I implore you, this season, to take caution with your every move. No...I must *insist* you do so. Your reckless ways have produced far too many casualties among the race of man."

"Sister," Apollo stated as he came to an abrupt halt, pausing just on the rim of a rather treacherous cliff, "I am always careful...well, to start I am, but then something happens along the way, and, well...perhaps you are right. Perhaps I do need to learn a bit of self-control."

"Just a bit," Artemis agreed, joining her brother upon the stone formation that extended before them as she adjusted her buckskin wrap, ever so slightly, so that her pert, full breasts were modestly covered once again.

"But I cannot help myself sometimes," Apollo lamented, looking more like an admonished child than a strapping, young man. "They are just so stimulating and..."

"Tasty. I know," Artemis interjected, with a roll of her dark eyes. "And, look, speak of them and they shall appear."

Apollo, following the length of her extended arm, shifted his gaze to far below where several, spectacular specimens could be seen frolicking in the burbling, lively tidal pools along the shoreline. As if on queue, the clouds above parted and nearly dissolved, allowing the full light and warmth of the sun to wash over the scene.

The stage was set.

"Go, have your fun, dear brother, for I have matters of

my own to tend to. However, please, heed my advice and be careful. Others are not as understanding as I. Yes, most of those boys down there have lived through nineteen or twenty mortal years, but they are still considered by some to be rather impressionable."

"Yes, I understand and I will...try, yes, try to behave myself," Apollo muttered in an attempt to appease his sibling, hoping his words would sound sincere enough so that she would continue on her way.

"Brother," was all he heard as a response, and he couldn't tell from the tone in her voice, as she moved on, if she really believed him or not. Regardless, he decided to proceed. These samples of manhood were far too dazzling not to partake of them.

Propelling himself over the edge, Apollo swiftly made his way down to the beach below where the boys were shamelessly toying with one another. He spied, from behind a boulder, as several of them now practiced their grappling moves upon the sandy beach – completely nude – while others continued to splash about in the natural pools. Their lean, strapping young bodies practically called to him, begging to be explored.

Without another thought, he undid the already loose knot found at his waist, allowing the flimsy cloth, which was barely covering his throbbing scepter and firm buttocks, to fall to the ground. Stepping out onto the beach, Apollo gracefully made his way toward the gathering of young men. He couldn't wait to be in their company.

Almost at once, each youth stopped mid-action and gave their full attention to the god. How could they not? He was simply radiant. Far more beautiful than any other living creature they had ever seen. It was as if a little piece of the sun had fallen to earth, he was that brilliant.

Apollo's flawless, smooth skin virtually glowed, which only helped to enhance every nook and crevice his perfectly shaped muscles created as they rippled and rolled with every step he took. His hair, the color and texture of gold and bronze silk, danced upon the ocean breeze, billowing around his gorgeous face, caressing his sun kissed cheeks. His eyes, brighter than the crystal-clear blue of the nearby waters, keenly darted about, drinking in the delicious feast of flesh set before him. However, it was his fully charged, insanely generous manhood that drew the most attention, followed by the massive pair of fleshy orbs dangling from below. On any other individual the entire package would've appeared outrageously obscene, but on Apollo it was simply spectacular – and he knew it.

"Good morning," he cooed as he made his way through the collection of boys, drinking in their bodies and scents, subtly brushing against them when the opportunity presented itself. "Care if I join you?"

There were no objections uttered, granted there were no words spoken at all since each boy was thrown a bit back, stunned into absolute silence. All eyes were locked firmly on Apollo's tempting manhood as it swung between his toned thighs. It was mesmerizing the way it heavily swayed back and forth, occasionally bouncing off of the massive sac that neatly rested below it.

"Now, boys, is this how you properly welcome a guest?" Apollo purred, swiftly approaching the one boy who appeared to have the willpower enough to meet his lustful gaze.

"No, Sir, it is not," the dark-haired boy responded, offering his hand as a greeting.

"There we go…," Apollo warmly noted, with a dazzling smile, as he moved closer to the boy, slowly extending his own hand. However, just before the two were about to exchange a friendly handshake, Apollo proceeded to buck his narrow hips, causing his throbbing rod to flop right into the open palm of the boy's hand.

Remaining completely composed, the boy simply grasped the fleshy tool presented to him. Apollo, at first, chuckled and

16

then, surprisingly, he found himself expelling a pleasure-filled sigh as the boy proceeded to skillfully work his thick, throbbing member up and down.

Neither uttered a word, as the youth continued to stroke, however, the lustful look in both of their eyes spoke volumes. Apollo, fully charged now, wanted nothing more than to take this boy and ravage him, but now was not the time or place, not with the others watching so intently.

Laughing a light, gentle laugh, Apollo suddenly withdrew himself from the young man's skilled hands and promptly turned his back to him. Facing the gathering of eager boys, he calmly addressed them, taking note of their bright, hopeful eyes and swiftly hardening cocks. "Well, it seems I have found myself a match. Therefore, the rest of you can retire for the day. Return in a day or two and perhaps, just perhaps, I will select one of you for a bit of amusement as well. However, at this time, on this day, you must abandon all hope of experiencing my heavenly body."

Dawdling, the disappointed boys slowly took their leave. With longing glances, they made their way off of the beach, giving Apollo his desired privacy. Though, as they proceeded, there were excited whispers and murmurs exchanged regarding what the future would bring for one of them.

"Well, now that it is just the two of us...," Apollo began as he turned to once again face the young man he had selected, "...we will have ourselves a scintillating romp, filled with..." However, as these last words fell from his mouth, he suddenly found himself awestruck, for standing before him was not the bold, handsome young man, but instead the goddess of love.

"Aphrodite?" Apollo questioned, foolishly glancing around her spectacular, curvaceous form, searching for the boy.

"In the flesh, although, not as boldly as some," she mused, taking in the sight of Apollo's generous, throbbing manhood.

"What have you done with the boy?" he demanded, attempting to ignore her licentious gaze.

"What boy?" she coyly replied, with an impious smile. "Do you mean this boy?"

Gracefully stepping aside, Aphrodite revealed *a* boy, but not *the* boy Apollo was looking for.

"Eros?" Apollo balked. "What are you doing here? What have you done with the boy who was here just a moment ago?"

On brilliant, feathered wings, the cherubic god of love fluttered toward Apollo and then proceeded to circle about his head. The disapproving expression he was clearly administering to the god was somewhat unsettling.

"You should take to heart the words and warnings of Artemis, dear Apollo," Eros began, "for she is a very wise woman."

"But...I do not understand," Apollo muttered, suddenly feeling exposed and a bit self-conscious.

"You cannot continue to toy with mortals as you just did and not pay a price," Aphrodite coolly interjected as she moved closer, lightly tapping his engorged rod with the tip of her index finger.

"My mother is correct," Eros confirmed as he continued to circle about Apollo's deliciously naked form. "How dare you flaunt yourself before a gathering of innocent young men and then swiftly dismiss the majority of them as if they were mere trinkets. Their hearts were shattered, Apollo, simply smashed to pieces by your careless, selfish actions."

"I...I did not imagine there would be much harm in having a little fun," Apollo muttered, hanging his head low, feeling ashamed.

"You must learn a lesson, dear boy, a lesson in discipline," the god of love informed him as he drew his glowing, golden

18

bow from his shoulder.

Apollo, knowing all too well what was about to happen, looked to Aphrodite for some help; however, at this point, the goddess of love wore a critical look upon her striking face, adding "I could not agree more, my dear."

Watching just long enough to see Eros draw an arrow from his quiver, Apollo quickly decided it was time to take action. He had no desire to lose his ability to love another – even if it was for only a day or two, which was the normal duration of being pricked by Eros's lead encased arrows. Whirling, Apollo swiftly bolted down the beach, away from both gods, attempting to put as much distance between them as possible. Cutting across the warm sand, he made his way back to the lofty cliff he came from. If he could get himself to the top and back into the forest, he could seek the assistance of his loving, understanding sister. If she was nowhere to be found, he would simply take cover. It would improve his odds greatly if he were not so exposed.

Pumping his lean, muscular legs, he couldn't help but notice how his erection remained in place. With each stride forward, his powerful manhood whacked against his inner thighs. His succulent, full balls bobbed about as well, swinging and colliding with his phallus. If he kept this up, he would most likely work himself into a panting, moaning frenzy, spewing a copious shower of pearlescent seed all over the landscape around him.

Leaping over the rim and landing on the edge of the fertile field that led to the dense forest, Apollo took a split second to access the progress of the others. Wildly scanning the rocky wall below, he saw no sign of either of them.

"How odd," Apollo noted, with a puzzled look on his handsome face, as he leaned over the edge to get a better look. However, in the instant it took him to mutter these two simple words, Eros had silently launched a volley of arrows, from high above, and swiftly made contact with Apollo's fully exposed, beautifully sculpted buttocks. One arrow, in particular, managed to capture a bull's eye.

"For the love of Zeus!" Apollo cried as he fell to his knees, cringing from the prickling sensation that was swiftly spreading over his defiled posterior. Immediately, his pulsating, massive prick deflated, withering down to an embarrassing scale. Even his plump testicles pulled in on themselves, nearly vanishing from sight.

Eros, smiling proudly, soared down from his position and took up a place next to Aphrodite who was now standing over Apollo's downed form.

"This is just a mere sample of what will happen to you each and every time you meddle in the affairs of mortals in such a careless style," noted the goddess of love as she bent to retrieve her son's arrows, violently plucking them from Apollo's reddening, slightly inflamed rear.

As Apollo's lean body jerked with each tug, he somehow mustered the control to hold back the nasty words he wished to cast at the two of them. He was already in enough trouble; he didn't need to foolishly add fuel to the fire.

"Do not look at us with such contempt, dear Apollo, for it is imperative that you change your ways or, as your sister already noted, there will continue to be far too many casualties as a result of your actions. You were lucky, on this particular day, that no mortal blood was shed. Your punishment would have been far more...unattractive, if there had been a single drop of red."

Turning away, Aphrodite motioned for Eros to follow her. Apollo watched as the two made their way back down to the beach. Lying on his stomach, giving his wounds time to heal, he took the moment to sort through the events of the last hour. Had what he done really affected the boys as Aphrodite claimed? Surely many of the gods toyed with mortals on many different levels, in many different ways – they had done it for hundreds of years and would probably continue to do so for many more to come – so why was he being singled out?

Feelings of anger and resentment started to take shape deep inside of him. Was he going to stand for such treatment? No. In two days time he would return to the beach, find the boy, and proceed with his original course of action. If Aphrodite or Eros showed, he would confront them and give them a piece of his mind. This was no way for a god to be treated.

However, history swiftly repeated itself, over and over, down to the very last detail of Apollo's cock and balls going from a stunning vision of majesty to a horrid appearance of malnourishment.

"We will do this time and time again, Apollo, until you change your ways," Aphrodite informed the golden-haired god, for the thirteenth time in three weeks. "You will learn to control yourself. You will learn the art of discipline, if not by my hand, then that of your fathers, for I will turn to him if you do not cease in your senseless quest to bed this particular boy."

Apollo, feeling the urge to cry, feeling downright ashamed of his inability to control his sexual desires, quietly removed himself from the goddess' presence.

"Know this, Apollo, my actions are driven by love," she whispered on the wind as he departed.

Returning several days later, Apollo stood on the rim of the cliff and watched the boys wrestle on the beach and splash about in the pools. He watched the handsome, dark-haired boy very closely, wondering what his thoughts were, wondering if he desired him the very same way. With each encounter, the boy appeared enamored with the god, but they were never able to take their venture much further because each time they attempted to Aphrodite and Eros abruptly intervened.

As Apollo continued to watch the boy, thinking shameless, dark thoughts about him, he became acutely aware of something. Glancing down, he found his usually rigid, aching manhood to be rather flaccid and well concealed by his cloth wrap.

"What is the meaning of this?" he spoke aloud to no

one in particular. "What has happened to me?" he cried out, wondering why the sight of the boy, as well as the images in his head, was not producing the normal reaction in his loins.

"Perhaps your heart has moved on," a stoic voice noted from just behind him.

Turning, with his limp cock in his hand, Apollo flushed with slight embarrassment as he realized it was his sister, Artemis, who stood with him. Swiftly covering himself, he shyly nodded in agreement.

"Look, it appears your dark-haired beauty has also moved on," she noted, pointing to the beach below. "His heart has continued on a different path."

The god watched as the young man distanced himself from the other boys on the beach. Slowly, with care, he moved along the shoreline and – to Apollo's surprise – proceeded to engage in a private meeting with a nubile, golden-haired, young woman.

"Well, I guess Aphrodite must have known what was best for him all along," Apollo firmly noted as he turned to face his sister who looked upon him with great compassion.

"Yes, I suppose she did," Artemis agreed, then added, "however, did she know what the best course of action was for you? I am not so certain of that. Your cravings for mortal flesh need to be fulfilled, not denied. It is part of who you are, dear brother."

"But, sister, you yourself said I needed to be more careful when it came to the affairs of man!"

"Yes, I implored you to be cautious, not entirely chaste."

"Well, then, perhaps I need to find a golden-haired distraction of my own," Apollo boldly stated, with one last glance to the boy and his new paramour. "Although, to be honest, I have always been more attracted to the dark-haired specimens. The Spartan's, in particular, have always held my interest."

"Oh, brother...," was all Apollo heard uttered by his sister as he sprinted off with a far lighter heart. "Here we go again," was what he would have heard on the tale-end of that sentence if he hadn't departed so quickly.

The Music Lesson

Written by: Nicholas Bowman

I am a busker, a troubadour, a street musician.

Guitar in hand, I stand on the corner, behind an open gig bag holding promo CDs you can buy, a mailing list you can join, and picture postcards with my Web address you can take.

And there's still plenty of room left over for donations, if you're so inclined.

In the greater scheme of things, I'm somewhere between a panhandler and a prostitute. I play for you. I don't expect to get something for nothing. But more often than not, I'm giving something for nothing. I haven't yet figured out how to get paid before I put out.

Although I have learned how to play the audience.

Twenty-something's want original material. They want to be the first to discover new talent. Baby boomers want covers of 60's and 70's standards. They want to remember the past they think they had. Seniors who like to go to rehearsals at Lincoln Center want flamenco. Ladies who attend matinees on Broadway want "A Wand' ring Minstrel I". And folkies of all ages like traditional songs and ballads.

Gay audiences can be lucrative. But they're as likely to tip because they like your body as they are because they like your music. I'm not proud. I put two to three hours in the gym a day six days a week. I play shirtless whenever I can.

As much BoBo as gay, the people going to and from the Hell's Pantry Flea Market certainly work that way. The bunch of us who play along Ninth Avenue weekend mornings can get more than just pocket change for our performances.

We space ourselves out so as not to crowd the shoppers or one another. Despite purchases or social commitments, some shoppers like to make as much a circuit of the regular musicians as they do of the regular dealers in the market. The shoppers are good for one or two dollars each – ten or twenty if they think you're cute or you'll put up with a quick grope. After a while you get to know who tips what and often even why.

Take the guy we call The Impresario. He's older, very well-groomed, and regardless of the season always well-dressed, more Paul Stuart than Brooks Brothers. His features are pleasant, but unmemorable, and framed by dark hair just graying at the temples – a touch too distinguished to be real, but at least it looks like a first-rate dye-job. His face is unlined and his skin tone and color are good, remaining untanned even in height of the summer. He keeps his height/weight proportional – by no definition is he overweight.

He visits the flea market every Sunday, but if he's ever bought anything, he must have had it delivered. But whatever he does or doesn't do there, he always makes a full circuit of the street musicians afterwards.

The Impresario listens to each one of us in turn, not just for a minute or two, but sometimes for as long as five minutes. Sometimes he even comes back for a second earful. His tendency to look people directly in the eye could be disconcerting, if not actually threatening. But when you play on the street, you get used to all types.

At some point, he drops a $50-bill into the hat and suggests that the performer put it toward music, singing, or composition lessons. An aspiring bluesman, for example, got a $50 and was told to take singing lessons before he ruined his vocal chords.

I've yet to get a $50. The closest I came was when The Impresario noticed my brand. Usually I get comments about New Orleans or The Three Musketeers, even when I'm wearing my je-me-souviens T-shirt. The Impresario asked about Louis XIV and Lully.

It took me a moment to remember even a bit of Lully, and I picked it out on my guitar. The Impresario was more impressed that I knew who Lully was, let alone could play a bit, than he was with the actual playing. I thought I'd scored the $50 for sure that Sunday. But all I got was a comment about its being hard to remember every note of every piece you've ever played.

I didn't bother to add Lully to my repertoire for him, but he paid more attention to me anyway. Or maybe it was just the fleur de Lis. If he knew the period, and I assumed he did, it was likely he knew what such a brand meant.

Since neither he nor I kept a rigid schedule, it was not too surprising that in good weather he'd find me either still wearing my shirt or with shirt already off. He once made a comment about my tattoo being the sort of political statement you regret once you reach 40. Something he'd know more about than I.

The weekend of Bastille Day was definitely a shirt-off day. The Impresario walked by while I was stripping. Maybe it was how my body was moving, but he noticed the scars on my back for the first time.

"Sjambok?" he asked.

I hid my surprise at his ability to identify the source of the marks.

"Something like that," I mumbled.

He changed his tone and his attitude. "You need that kind of corrections, boy."

Automatically, I lowered my head and my gaze as I put on my baseball cap and adjusted the visor to shield my eyes from the sun. "Everyone needs a bit of discipline and direction in his life."

"You obviously do, boy."

"Yes, Sir," I said. "I do, Sir."

I put on my shades while he looked at my crotch. I could feel my cock expand, stretching my jeans, almost as if it were being drawn into his stare.

He pulled a card case out of his jacket pocket and took out a card, which he tossed into my gig bag. As he slid the case back into his pocket he said, "See you at 4 p.m., boy. Don't be late."

"Sir."

I picked up my guitar, adjusted the strap, and went back to playing.

He continued along the circuit. I think he gave a female contortionist the $50. Perhaps she struck a sour note with him.

I had mixed feelings about The Impresario. There is something about an authority figure who assumes responsibility to execute the punishment appropriate for what I did or did not do that reaches deep into my core. If it's a cop/suspect, guard/prisoner, or executioner/convict scenario, so much the better.

And he certainly struck a chord when he said corrections in the plural and picked up on my line about discipline and direction. It was clear enough he planned to hand out the punishment I deserved.

On the other hand, I had been a little too fast and a little too casual in taking a submissive stance. I didn't really know who he was or what I would be letting myself in for if I turned up at four. I have a history of asking for more than I want and getting more than I asked for. And the scars to prove it.

On the third hand, it had been close to a month since I'd last been punished like the piece of shit I am. I was feeling mentally grungy.

But at six foot and 175 pounds, I probably could hold my own against a man 30 years older and six inches shorter even if I had let him begin to assume psychological dominance over me.

After the crowds thinned out in the mid-afternoon, I pulled The Impresario's card from my bag. It said he was Martin Gruen and lived in the Upper West Side.

The name was vaguely familiar. By the time I finished packing up – really just the instrument since I play on a flamenco guitar; the brighter, more percussive sound can hold its own against moderate street noise and I don't have to be bothered with stuff like wires, amplifiers, and battery packs – I placed him. A Martin Gruen had produced a popular series of music instruction books for children. I remembered having to work my way through one of them when I was a kid.

I shouldered my bag and hopped an uptown train. It was probably going to be OTK with a bare hand followed by corner time or a schoolmarmish lecture or both. Better than nothing.

The apartment house was one of those 100-year-old block-sized buildings for which the Upper West Side is well-known. I stuffed my cap and my sunglasses into a pocket of my gig bag while the doorman announced me.

I got off the elevator with the heavy feeling of impending doom tickling my belly. The rush of risk was kicking in.

I knocked on the door.

It opened immediately.

"You know why you're here, boy."

No preliminaries. The Impresario just looked right into my eyes and spoke with a cold, controlled anger. I felt his dominance wash over me as I entered boy space.

"Yes, Sir," I mumbled.

"Get in here, boy. Right now."

He grabbed my ear and pulled me inside.

"Take your clothes off, boy."

"Yes, Sir.

I lowered my guitar gently to the floor of the foyer.

"Now, boy. Stop stalling and start stripping."

"Yes, Sir."

I stripped while The Impresario radiated impatience. But how long does it take to pull off a T-shirt, push off a pair of Vans, and drop a pair of jeans, which was all I was wearing? Unless you count my belt, which was unlikely to come into play.

The Impresario remained clothed: a pink button-down shirt, with an open collar and rolled up sleeves; grey cotton trousers; and red-brown Weejuns. I just bet his boxers were baggy and his socks were over-the-calf.

I dropped my clothes on top of my guitar and stood with my head bent, feet shoulder width apart, and wrists crossed behind my back.

He looked at my piercing.

"You're going to feel a lot more pain than you did getting that thing, boy," he said.

"Yes, Sir," I said. "I know, Sir."

He looked up. "The necklace, boy."

He held his hand out.

I took off my pendent and dropped it into his hand. He tossed it onto the pile of clothes on top of my bag. The only way I could feel more naked and exposed would be if he asked me to take the ampallang out of my dick head.

The Impresario grabbed my ear again and pulled me into the apartment. The main room was a cool and understated masterpiece of the interior designer's craft, centered on a fireplace and a grand piano.

He dragged me across the room and down a hall, while telling me that I knew what I did, that he wouldn't be doing this if I didn't deserve it.

He pulled me ahead of him and half pushed me into a music room.

There was another piano, some wind instruments, and a drum set. A range of stringed instruments – lutes, guitars, mandolins, and the like – were mounted on the walls along with the covers of every edition of every instructional manual he ever produced. The Impresario *was* that Martin Gruen.

All but one of the two dozen or so bentwood café chairs was lined up along the walls. The exception was in the center, next to a music stand on which were draped three leather guitar straps, ranging from soft and supple to stiff and solid.

This could be intense.

"Well, boy, what are you waiting for? You knew this was coming. And you know what you did to deserve it."

That I did.

I walked over to the chair and paused behind it to adjust my feet to be slightly wider than my shoulders before I bent over the back and grabbed the seat from the sides.

"You know you earned this, boy."

"Yes, Sir."

As I lowered my head until it almost touched the seat, Mr. Gruen set the metronome for three-quarter time.

"And it's not about what turns you on, boy."

"No, Sir." Actually, my dick was nice and respectful: full, but not hard. "It's not, Sir."

Jack-knifed over the back of the chair, bottom up, I couldn't see him, of course, but I felt the strap as soon as it hit my bottom. It was a right hand forehand right on the beat of the metronome. The next strike was a backhand, also to the beat of the metronome.

He continued keeping time to the beat of the metronome. HARD forehand soft backhand soft forehand HARD backhand soft forehand soft backhand. He was using the softest of the three leather guitar straps, but after every few bars he increased the intensity of the strikes, which with the steady, relentless rhythm was having its effect on me. I could feel my cock and balls bounce from every third strike.

There is no way I could know what was going through Mr. Gruen's mind while he strapped me, but he went on about responsibility, holding me accountable, and betraying talent and tradition.

I focused on my feelings of guilt and shame,

embarrassment and humiliation, from everything I ever did wrong, real or imagined. I slipped into feeling powerless and very small.

But Mr. Gruen kept on, HARD stroke soft stroke soft stroke HARD stroke soft stroke soft stroke. I began to gasp and gripped the seat harder to stop from clenching my teeth. I wasn't turned off, but began to wonder if I'd have to bear the embarrassment of not being able to take my punishment.

Then Mr. Gruen paused.

"You know I wouldn't do this, boy, if I didn't respect your talent."

"Yes, Sir."

He re-set the metronome to two-four time.

"But you have to start respecting your own talent, boy."

"Yes, Sir," I said. "I promise to do better, Sir."

"You know this is for your own good, boy."

"Yes, Sir."

I knew he switched to a heavier strap the moment it hit my bottom. It was a light slap, but it really stung on my tenderized bottom. Furthermore it was a left hand forehand. Mr. Gruen was making sure my bottom was blistered from both sides and all angles.

He also reversed the order again and again. A strong forehand was followed by a soft backhand which was followed by a strong backhand which was followed by a soft forehand.

Mr. Gruen started with soft strikes but built intensity again. It was relentless. ONE two ONE two ONE two. My cock was bobbing from the impact and occasionally the edge of the belt would hit the back of my balls.

I howled and gasped. But whether it was accidentally

or "accidentally", Mr. Gruen used the blows to talk about how in the age of Lully and Louis XIV boys were castrated to keep their minds and bodies focused on their music.

He kept going. I was yelping with just about every blow. I began to choke. If he kept this up, I would break down and cry. I didn't know what Mr. Gruen would do to me if I suddenly got real hard and shot my load while he was talking about cutting my balls off.

He broke his pattern with eight hard strikes of the strap and then paused again.

I was breathing heavily, all but gasping for breath.

"I just don't think you're getting the message, boy."

"I am, Sir. I'm sorry, Sir. Really, truly sorry, Sir. Scout's honor, Sir."

He set the metronome for four-four time.

"As if you were a boy scout."

"Actually, I was a boy scout."

"Then act like one."

The heaviest strap hit my bottom. It was light but I half gasped half howled anyway, with only the endorphins to keep my cock up.

He still kept to the beat, but switched hands every few measures. Hard right forehand soft right backhand soft right forehand soft right forehand hard left forehand soft left backhand soft left forehand soft left forehand. Each set of blows a little stronger than the last. Usually somewhere on my bottom, but still catching the back of my balls from time to time.

I broke. I screamed. I cried. "Please, Sir. I'll be good, Sir. I promise, Sir."

But the blows kept coming. ONE two three four. ONE

two three four.

"I'm sorry, Sir. I know I fucked up. I'll do better, Sir.

But the blows kept coming. ONE two three four. ONE two three four.

"I know I'm a fuck-up, Sir. But I can learn to respect the music, Sir. I promise, Sir."

But the blows kept coming. ONE two three four. ONE two three four.

"Sir," I wailed, "I'm sorry. Really sorry. I won't do it again, Sir."

Mr. Gruen stopped.

"That's better, boy."

And then he hit me eight times hard and fast.

"But we don't use words like 'fuck' around here, do we, boy."

"No, Sir. We don't, Sir. Sorry, Sir."

"Get up, boy."

"Thank you, Sir."

I straightened up and turned around to face him as he turned off the metronome. I kept my head bowed, my feet apart, and my wrists crossed behind my back.

"Thank you, Sir. I appreciate your making the time and effort to make me see the light of day, Sir."

"Now you know the proper way to say 'thank you', don't you, boy."

"Sir."

He tapped his belt buckle.

"Now you know the proper way to say 'thank you', don't you, boy."

Now I did. "Yes, Sir."

I kneeled, keeping my hands behind me. It's not as if I don't identify as a cock sucking faggot. And at least I wasn't going to be face fucked eight to the bar. A boogie-woogie blow job is just so not me.

Mr. Gruen unzipped his trousers and pulled out his cock and balls. His cock was a mouth-watering, sphincter-twitching thick eight incher, easily topping mine by an inch and a quarter. Cut, unfortunately; but you could say that about mine as well. His balls were egg-sized low-hangers.

As we Buddhists might say, when you eat, you eat; when you shit, you shit; and when you suck cock, you suck cock. I began to thank Mr. Gruen properly.

I mixed it up. I tapped my tongue on the head and the shaft; licked both and the rim of the corona as well; worked my way through the alphabet with my tongue on his balls; came down on him half-way, all the way, and just the head.

We were both getting pretty hard.

But the strap kept landing on my upper back again and again. Mr. Gruen seemed to be determined to hit the same spots over and over again. I would have some interesting welts to go with scar tissue.

More difficult was to keep from clenching my jaw or bighting down every time the strap hit. Sinking my teeth into Mr. Gruen's cock would not be a good idea, especially since he kept making such comments as "Is that the best you can do, boy?" or "Don't you know how to suck cock, boy?"

Then the whipping stopped.

"I'm going to cum, boy."

And he exploded into my mouth.

Mr. Gruen pulled out. He looked wobbly, but after a moment he steadied himself and tucked his cock and balls back inside his trousers.

He looked down and saw my wood.

"You're hard, boy."

"Yes, Sir."

"You want to cum, boy?"

"Yes, Sir. May I please cum, Sir?"

"Good, boy. You're learning. Only I decide whether you may cum or not. Get up, boy."

I got up slowly so that I could keep my balance while keeping my hands behind my back. My cock stayed angled up and out, the steel knobs of the ampallang shining brightly against the swollen head, looking like an angry reptile.

"You may jerk-off in the bathroom, boy. There's a shower, if you want it."

"Yes, Sir. Thank you, Sir."

"It's across the hall."

He followed me into the bathroom, stopping in the doorway.

The bathroom was also well-designed. The shower included floor to ceiling clear glass doors. Showtime.

"How do you clean that thing, boy?"

"It cleans itself, Sir. It crosses the pee-hole. Your piss is... "

"Yes, I know that, boy." He paused for a moment. "And if you do have to piss, remember to sit. Only men stand."

"Yes, Sir."

Mr. Gruen kept his eye on me as I adjusted the temperature of the water; got in; soaped up slowly; worked my cock; shot my load; watched it spiral down the drain; and rinsed off. I turned the water off and got out.

He tossed a towel at me.

"Throw it in the hamper when you're done, boy."

"Yes, Sir."

He walked off.

I dried off – and remembered to throw the towel in the hamper – and took a leak – and remembered to sit. Then I wandered out of the bathroom to reclaim my clothes and my guitar.

Mr. Gruen was looking at my guitar from all angles. It is handmade, but not by a "name" luthier. It took me a moment to realize that he had changed the strap to the heaviest one he used to beat me.

"Spanish, but not Spanish," he said. "Portuguese?"

"Close, Sir. It was made in Brazil."

"Ah. That explains your technique. Or perhaps your technique explains your guitar."

He put it carefully back into the bag.

"Your clothes are over there, boy."

"Over there" was the coffee table. I dressed while he fastened the bag.

"You'll be using my strap, boy, so that when you play, you'll remember I'm keeping an eye on you."

"Yes, Sir. Thank you, Sir."

It wasn't until I got home that I realized Mr. Gruen had also confiscated my old strap. Unless I wanted to go out and buy a new one, I had no choice but to use the one he gave me. It was both creepy and comforting. The thought made me hard.

I sent him a note thanking him for both the strap and the strapping.

As for the strap, I used it. I was very aware of what it had done to me for the first couple of days, but that passed about the same time as the last of the welts. By the end of the week, all I was aware of was who used it on me. It really was just like having Mr. Gruen watch over me.

Of course, I wore the strap the next Sunday at the flea market. It would have been disrespectful not to, if I had the choice.

Of course, Mr. Gruen came by, making his usual rounds. He gave me a hard look every time he passed by, but waited until he caught me taking a break before he spoke.

"You clearly haven't learned your lesson, boy."

"I'm sorry, Sir. I'm trying the best that I can, Sir."

"Just trying isn't good enough, boy."

"I know, Sir. I'll try harder, Sir."

"You'll report to me at 4 p.m., boy. And you won't just try, you'll be there. Won't you, boy?"

"Yes, Sir. I will, Sir. Four p.m., Sir."

Spanked by my Landlord's Son

Written by: Christopher Trevor

The knock at my apartment door came around twenty after six PM, ten minutes after I had arrived home on that Friday night. At this point in time I would call that the most fateful Friday night of my damned life. In twenty-six years I had never known a more eventful night let me tell you. Stripped out of my office suit (what I sometimes refer to as my monkey suit) and tie down to my navy blue GoldToe brand nylon calf length wide ribbed dress socks and a pair of frosty white Calvin Klein boxer briefs I padded from my bedroom out toward the kitchen calling "Yeah, who is it?" as whoever the fuck it was knocked insistently. I figured it was more than likely just some religious nut that had been to see the landlord and was now going to try his door to door wiles on yours truly here. It seemed to me that it was always around the damned holidays that these religious mojo's found their way out of the woodwork and to the doors of busy people to hand out their insane paraphernalia. If there was a need to open the door I figured I would just quickly pull my suit trousers back on...or so I figured. If it was, as I suspected just someone bringing nonsense to my door I would just send them on their way by telling them how not interested I was in whatever cause they were promoting.

"Who is it?" I called out again.

"It's Vinny Mr. Brego," I heard my muscle headed landlord's son call out to me in response from outside my apartment door. "You know Mr. and Mrs. Giordano's son."

"Ah jeez," I whispered and looked down at my scantily clad self. *"Fuck, fuck, fuck..."*

I quickly thought to dash back to my bedroom and get my suit trousers back on but then changed my mind. Countless fucking times I had seen Vinny the muscle head barely dressed while he worked out in the back yard of the house where I rented a one bedroom apartment, directly upstairs from him and his old-world minded Italian parents. The twenty-something year old bodybuilder seemed to love showing off for the neighborhood in the backyard in his skimpy posing trunks while he flexed his huge muscles and lifted what seemed like tons on his weight benches. It amazed me that he was never charged with indecent exposure. It was where my one bedroom apartment was concerned that I knew why Vinny was at my door. Usually it was his Italian accented dad who came knocking and hollering whenever I was late with the rent, which was pretty much all the time. ("Pat, you uh late with the rent again!" Vinny's Italian accented dad would rant in my handsome mug. "If you a late again with a my money I a trow you outa here!") But Vinny's dad and mom were presently in old Italy, visiting with some relatives or whatnot. So this time out it fell to Vinny, their overly muscled son to come knocking and collect the monthly payment from me. I took Vinny to be as ignorant as his dad and mom, figured he would be just as easy to bamboozle with a sob story or two.

"Yeah, yeah, I'm coming Vinny!" I called out loudly, scratching my crotch through my boxer briefs.

Vinny was the last thing on my mind at that moment let me tell you, because within an hour and a half I was going to be out on a date with a very hot and very beautiful young lady. As I thought of her and scratched my crotch my horse-sized cock shifted and stiffened a bit in my boxer briefs. I had had my eye on this lady, Linda her name was for some time at that point. We had met on the train on the way to work. She was new in the neighborhood, lived alone and when she started taking the same train that I take every morning was when we started chatting a bit. It took me two weeks to get up the nerve to ask her out for dinner on a Friday night. I swear when I saw her it was almost like love at first sight. She has chestnut brown long hair and beautiful piercing dark eyes. When I first saw her I thought she looked a bit like a famous actress. In her business attire of tight skirt and loose fitting blouse (with delicious looking tits I might add) and high heels she looked totally sexy yet real classy at the same time on that subway platform I got to say. She did not have a hair out of place and she was breathtakingly gorgeous with just a hint of makeup on. While we talked and got to know each other a bit I told her that I worked as a computer systems analyst for Chaser bank and she told me she was a marketing director for a jewelry company. When I finally got up the nerve to ask her out and she said yes I was totally ecstatic. I could not believe it but it seemed that the girl of my dreams had moved right into my neighborhood. And now the night had come and I had to contend with the landlord's idiot son at my door, jeez! Well, I figured I would tell him the facts of life of how my Friday night was shaping up and send him on his way, hardy, har, har fellas! Once the muscle bound dork heard my sexy plans for the evening I was sure he would come knocking another time for his money, or so I thought. I figured I would just give the mutton-headed Vinny some kind of sob story, send him on his workout way and then get out of my boxer briefs and socks and into a shower before my upcoming hot date. As Vinny knocked harder I stepped to the door and opened it. He stood there in a pair of red cotton gym shorts, a white muscle tee shirt and sneakers with ankle length white sweat socks. The muscles in his bowling-ball-sized biceps seemed to be rippling.

43

I guessed he had been working out earlier and decided to come knocking now. Heaven forbid that the kid should miss his scheduled workout. His legs were like two tree-trunks, thick and muscular, well toned. With his nearly black eyes peering angrily at me he took in the sight of me as I stood before him in just my boxer briefs and dress socks.

"Do you always come to your door in just your underpants and socks Brego?" the landlord's son asked me, sneering at my near nakedness.

I decided to ignore his snide remark and just move on quickly as to why he was there, as if I didn't know. It always amazed me how he had no Italian accent like his old-world minded parents did.

"Yeah Vinny, what can I do for you?" I asked the guy, nearly laughing as I took in the sight of the fact that he now sported a crew cut hair style, high and tight almost.

I guessed that he fancied himself a marine or something like that now, hardy fucking har.

"Don't play all dumb with me Pat," Vinny said with a sneer, stepping past me and into my apartment.

"Uh, I don't recall inviting you in buddy," I said, turning and facing him, me still standing in the doorjamb.

"Hmm, funny, I don't recall you paying this month's rent," Vinny said in response. "So with that in mind I would have to say that being that I'm the landlord's son *I can* come in here whenever the fuck *I want*!"

His man-sized nipples were showing and were very erect and pronounced looking at the sides of his muscle style string tee-shirt. For some damned and fucked up reason my stiff cock churned a bit at the sight of those man-sized tits of his. I quickly reasoned it was tits and I was a fool for them. I thought of Linda's tits and how they would make for good eating later that night.

"Alright look, Vinny, I'm a little backed up on my bills this month..." I began, pasting a dumb guy look on my handsome mug, trying to reason with the idiotic stack of muscles.

"Why should this month be any different from other months?" Vinny shot back angrily at me and I felt my toes curl back in my gold toes socks.

"If I had a nickel for every time my father had to come here looking for the rent check," Vinny went on, stepping closer to me, nearly in my face now. "Well, let me tell you Patty boy, I'm not my father! So, if you want to continue living here and continue paying the cheap ass rent that my parents charge you starting tonight you'll have your rent on time. If not you can pay the consequences and go live somewhere else!"

The way he was in my face and the way he had called me "Patty boy" had really riled me, pissed me off to be totally honest here. Patty boy? Where in hell did he come off addressing me in such a condescending manner?

"Look, Vinny, I'm sorry, I really am," I said, trying to keep my anger in check.

Built and muscular as I am Vinny obviously outweighed, out-muscled and out-towered me by more than a few inches and most definitely more than a few inches of brawn on his well-toned and well-developed body.

"But look, there's no fucking way I can get you your rent money tonight," I said, trying to sound as reasonable as possible, regretting that I had used the "F" word, jeez.

"Why not?" he asked, looking me up and down, really taking in the sight of me in my navy blue dress socks and white boxer briefs. "Just get back into that expensive suit I saw you had on when you came home earlier and go to the ATM machine at the bank and..."

"I would love to buddy, I really would," I said, stepping closer to him and giving one of his upper arms a fast and friendly squeeze.

Jeez, his arm felt like there was iron under his soft silky skin...

"But you see, tonight I cannot do that, I most definitely cannot, *cannot* do that tonight Vinny my man, so it'll have to be tomorrow, first thing in the morning," I said, sounding very promising, although I knew I was full of shit here.

"And why the fuck not?" Vinny asked, glancing down at the spot on his arm where I had squeezed it, a look almost of disgust on his ruggedly handsome puss.

"Well, tonight I have a date, a *really* hot date," I said by way of explanation, a grin on my face as I spoke. "And I really, *really* need to get ready for that date Vinny boy."

I figured that the way he lived his life at home, working out nearly every minute of everyday the muscle-stack would have no idea just how much a hot date meant to a guy like me. With that I stepped around him and he turned facing me now, his back to the open door of my apartment. The huge muscles in his chest were causing his pecs to bounce; involuntarily it seemed at that...his man-sized tits jutted up a tad more with the muscle-motion, sexy somehow, even though he was a guy. It seemed to me that his anger was somehow making his tits engorge.

"So, if you would be so kind as to be on your way," I said, still grinning and now pointing at the door. "I will have your money for you tomorrow. Now I need to shower and get dressed for my date..."

I saw the look of outright rage on his face and I loved it.

"Please close the door behind you on your way out buddy," I snickered.

I turned my back on him and began padding on my socked feet toward the bathroom when suddenly I heard a guttural sound come from my landlord's son.

"You son of a bitch," he snarled as he sidled up behind me, one well muscled arm outstretched, his fingers hooked into claws as he reached toward my head. "Patronize me will you? Like I said Patty boy, I'm not my dad!"

As I reeled around to face him once again and to get his muscled ass out of my apartment he grabbed my right-sided earlobe in a death-grip between his thumb and first two fingers of his right hand. He had snagged my earlobe before I could turn to face him...

"OWWWWW! HOLY FUCKING shit you asshole!" I reeled loudly as he yanked me back by my earlobe, hefting me nearly to my socked toes, me wobbling a bit.

"Asshole huh?" Vinny asked me, twisting my lobe in his fingers and thumb, my arms thrashing uselessly at my sides. "You call me asshole I'll call you ass-wipe. How's that sound Patty boy? *You're the wipe that'll wipe my asshole!*"

"AAARRRHHH JEEZ, get your meaty hands off me you stupid muscle boy," I seethed. "I told you I would have your goddamned money for you tomorrow. Now tonight I got a date waiting for me and..."

As I spoke he yanked again on my earlobe and I swear to Christ in his heaven that I thought for sure he was going to tear my ear right off the side of my head.

"I got news for you ass-wipe, your date tonight has just been canceled," Vinny said from behind me as he held tight to my ear and started moving me toward the door to my apartment. "I'll still get my dad's money tomorrow, but you're going to get yours tonight. Like I said you'll pay the consequences if you want to keep living here so cheaply! I suppose you don't recall me saying anything about you paying consequences huh Patty boy?"

"WHAT in the fuck do you mean my dates been canceled?" I ranted, trying to pry my ear out of his grip, but he just held on tighter.

47

Searing pain soared through me as the muscle-stack held my earlobe, twisted it and maneuvered me around on my socked feet with it. I felt as if I was a puppet and he was my goddamned puppeteer.

"Instead of a hot date with a hot lady Patty boy, you're going to be spending some time with me in my home-gym, *down in the basement,*" Vinny said from behind me as he plodded me toward the door to my apartment.

From the way he sounded I could tell that his teeth were clenched. I was afraid that if I pulled myself too hard in my attempts to break free of his grip I would wind up with just one ear.

"Fuck that shit you dumb overgrown kid," I rasped, my own teeth clenched as I tottered stupidly on my socked feet. "I'm not spending any time with you anywhere! Now let go of me and be on your way! Shit but that hurts, let go of my fucking ear man!"

But instead he gripped my earlobe tighter and I found myself walking unsteadily out the door of my apartment and into the hallway, in my damned underpants and socks! Holy shit and jeez!

"Patty boy, when I get done with you tonight you'll never be late with your rent again," Vinny said as he moved me toward the stairs, the stairs that led down to his and his parents home on the ground floor.

"Oh yeah?" I called back at him, holding onto the banister tightly with one hand as he forced me slowly down the stairs.

By now I couldn't even feel my earlobe as he held onto it...

"After this little spectacle of yours we'll see how long I stay living in this dump that you and your father call an apartment," I ranted and in response Vinny slammed me against the stair wall. "OWWWWWW! You fucker! Look, let me

48

get back in my apartment you asshole! I'm wearin' just my damned under shorts and dress socks here!"

"Not to worry ass-wipe, we're the only ones here tonight," Vinny said and almost laughed behind me. "Now move it patty boy!"

With that he pushed me along down the steps, step by painful step.

"OOWWWWWW! WHAT in the fuck are you planning on doing to me man?" I asked through the pain I was feeling in my head. "If you haven't realized it you just kidnapped me right out of my apartment!"

"Oh I plan to teach you Patty boy, I plan to teach you things like respect for your landlord, I plan to teach you about paying your bills on time," Vinny chided me. "I plan to teach you a lot of things tonight. And just for the record here, seeing as you haven't paid your rent yet, I did not kidnap you out of your apartment. I kidnapped you out of my apartment. Also, seeing as you haven't paid your rent as far as I'm concerned you were trespassing in that apartment! So you see Patty boy, I'm not just some dumb overgrown kid or muscle head, as you call me. NOW MOVE!"

"AAAYYYRRRR!" I screamed out pitifully as he twisted my earlobe and I stepped gingerly down and down the stairs. "Jeez man, my ear...be careful huh?"

When we reached the bottom of the stairs Vinny forced me through his parent's house by my ear and toward the basement stairs. I plodded along on immaculately clean linoleum floors and thick rugs as well. As he forced me down the second flight of stairs, those that led down to his basement/gym I again held tight to the banister. I feared losing my footing and possibly an ear as well if I fell from his grasp. When we were downstairs in the home/gym/basement Vinny finally let go of my ear. I was nearly crying as I rubbed it gently and he dashed up the stairs to lock the basement door, pocketing the key in his shorts pocket.

"Look man, whatever the hell you got in that muscled mind of yours you can just forget it," I said, holding up a finger as Vinny trotted back down the stairs. "You may be all hard and muscular body-wise but your brain is as soft as mush!"

I watched as he walked through the gym passing by various exercise machines, benches and apparatuses as he made his way back over to me where I stood on a thick rubber mat.

"In case you don't know it asshole what you just did was abusive to the tenant and it's kidnapping that you got me down here," I went on in my rant. "Whether or not I paid my rent you kidnapped me! I can have my lawyer sue the gym shorts off you for that shit!"

"Oh yeah Patty boy?" Vinny asked me, sauntered over to me and pushed me hard on my chest, easily sending me off balance and sprawling to the rubber mat.

"OOOFFFF..." I huffed as I hit the mat in a heap, landing painfully on my side.

"Prove it, ass-wipe," he chuckled and quickly went over to a wall where various sized racquet ball paddles hung.

He took one off the hook it was hanging on.

As I slowly got to my feet Vinny made his way quickly back over to me and with one mean kick at my legs sent me toppling to the rubber mat again.

"UHHHHH, you bastard," I seethed through clenched teeth as I hit the mat a second time.

"Tell me Patty boy, have you ever played racquet ball?" Vinny asked me and swung the paddle in the air, feigning a tennis player-like motion.

"Sure, who hasn't?" I replied and slowly pulled myself to my knees.

If the guy toppled me again I planned on bringing him

down with me this time, but I would soon find that Vinny the mutton muscle head had other plans for me while I was down there on the mat.

"Well, I'm going to play racquet ball right now Patty boy," Vinny said and again swung the paddle in the air, it making a whooshing sort of sound this time as he swung it mightily hard. "Only thing is, your ass is going to be the wall I bounce this paddle against...no need for a ball in this game!"

"WHA...WHAT?" I bellowed and this time as I started to pull myself to my feet Vinny reached down and grabbed a handful of my hair.

He yanked me upwards by my hair, HARD...

"OWWWWRRRRR, you sick fuck!" I screamed in a man's pain...

I came up on my tiptoes and once more my arms flailed uselessly at my sides as Vinny moved me along to where he wanted me.

"We'll look at this as the first part of the lessons I'll teach you tonight Patty boy," Vinny said as he paraded me through his home/gym by my hair. "Remember what I told you ass-wipe, I'm going to teach you a lot of things down here tonight."

First the muscle headed lunk had nearly torn my ear off me, now it felt as if he was planning to yank out a clump of my hair by the roots. A few times he kneed me in the ass to move me faster, pulling me along by my hair so hard that I thought *he would* literally tear it out by the roots. As I ranted and reeled crazily Vinny let go of me and pushed me bodily against a punching bag that hung from the ceiling. To keep from falling I threw my arms out in front of me and grabbed the punching bag. As I hugged onto it Vinny came up behind me and WHACKED me hard across the ass with his racquet ball paddle.

"YOWWWCCHHH, holy shit man!" I screeched. "WHAT

51

IN THE FUCK?"

As I let go of the punching bag and went to turn around and face Vinny he whaled his paddle against my ass yet again, the sound of it a loud WHACK!, sending me back against the punching bag, hugging it tight.

"OH HOLY FUCKING SHIT you dumb stack of muscles," I reeled, starting to feel real fear setting in along with my anger.

I clung tighter to the punching bag.

"Now, stay that way or I swear to God and all the angels in heaven that I'll tie you to that damned punching bag," Vinny seethed behind me and WHACKED my ass a third time with his racquet ball paddle.

"OWWWWWW, you fucking fucked up fucker!" I snarled and he WHACKED, WHACKED, and WHACKED my ass three times in fast succession.

The blows landed hard and stung like the devil...

"Come on Vinny, this isn't funny here, you're fucking spanking my ass!" I railed as I clung to the punching bag.

WHACK! WHACK! WHACK!, came three more ass reddening swipes from my landlord's son as he paddled my damned ass cheeks.

"Like I said Patty boy, you're going to pay the consequences, then you're going to pay your rent," Vinny said through a grin and stood in real close to me at my side. "Sometimes bad boys need to learn a lesson the old-fashioned way! Its something my father taught me growing up!"

I held the punching bag tight as he whaled whack after whack after whack on my underpants clad ass cheeks.

"AAAAWWWWWWW!" I screamed. "I swear man, I'm goin' to make you pay as well, and it won't be rent I'm talking here! SHIT!"

In response Vinny administered WHACK after awful whack to my sexy ass cheeks...

"Damn it all man, I'm being spanked like a little kid here..." I said miserably.

"Precisely ass-wipe," Vinny taunted me and whacked, whacked, whacked me again and again, his racquet ball paddle inscribing itself on my poor ass cheeks.

All I could do was hold on tight to that damned punching bag as Vinny stayed positioned behind me perfectly accurately, almost at a soldierly stance, whaling and slamming his racquet ball paddle harder and harder against the cheeks of my underpants clad ass.

WHACK, WHACK, WHACK, WHACK, the sound of Vinny's racquet ball paddle connecting with my buttocks was maddening...and not to mention how red my ass was starting to feel.

After a while I lost count of how many times the fucking guy had swatted my poor ass cheeks with his racquet ball paddle. All I knew was that my butt cheeks felt like they were on fire...

"Okay Patty boy, that's a good warm-up I would say," Vinny said and took a few steps away from me, the huge muscles in his arms flexing involuntarily it seemed. "Now for the next round I want those designers under shorts off you."

I reeled around facing him, my back to the punching bag and said in a high pitched tone of voice, "You have got to be kidding me!"

I saw the look of fierce determination in his eyes and knew in an instant that he was not kidding me.

"You can take those under shorts off yourself or I'll tear them off you Patty boy," Vinny said to me, looking almost hungrily it seemed to me at the chub I was surprisingly sporting in my damned under shorts.

"Jeez, hell of a way to refer to my designer boxer briefs, that's all I can say," I said stupidly and slowly shucked my underpants down to my socked ankles and stepped out of them.

My horse-sized cock was totally hard, the green veins in my shaft totally paramount, my succulent and juicy balls hung down real sexily in my sweaty sac and pre seed oozed from my piss slit. It was humiliating, to say the least how that goddamned dollop of pre-seed oozed from my slit and then dangled there for a few seconds before hitting the floor. I took a deep breath as Vinny chuckled at the sight of my engorged and pulsing manhood...

"You enjoying this Patty boy?" Vinny asked me and my cock twitched in fear. "Shit, it proves that an ass-wipe like you would benefit from an old-fashioned ass thrashing."

"Fuck you man, my cock is always hard," I replied with a smirk on my face. "Although I doubt that's something that a dumb muscle-head like you would know about..."

In response Vinny reeled around and SMACKED me hard across the jaw...

"HOOOFFFFFFF!" was the sound I made as I spun twice on my socked feet, wobbled stupidly, groped for the punching bag behind me, missed it horribly and landed on the floor of the gym this time.

Looking up through blurred vision I saw the punching bag swinging a bit back and forth over me. As I rubbed the spot on my jaw where I had been clocked I felt as if I had been hit by a truck, Vinny was that fucking strong buds. Then, I felt one of my socked ankles grabbed and I was dragged along the floor toward a chair...

In what seemed like no time whatsoever I found myself stretched out on my stomach over Vinny's lap, my hard cock wedged between his iron-like thighs and my hands tied at the wrists in front of me as they dangled downward. As I lay splayed on my landlord's son's lap he raised his arm high over and over and brought his racquet ball paddle crashing down hard over and over on my now naked and upturned ass.

"Okay ass-wipe this will now be part two of your lessons to be learned tonight," Vinny said to me, rubbing his paddle against my reddened ass cheeks in between swatting them.

"OWWWWWWW! You fucking schmuck! You can't do this to me man!" I bellowed and struggled to get my hands untied, noting stupidly that he had bound my wrists with a goddamned workout style jump rope. "RRRRRRRRRRR GAWD!"

Each swat to my poor ass cheeks was worse than the one before it. I somehow had the feeling that an egg could be fried on my ass, that's how red Vinny had it already. And the fucking stupid muscle head wasn't even done with me yet.

WHACK, WHACK, WHACK, WHACK, WHACK, went Vinny's racquet ball paddle against my ass cheeks as the guy held my cock tight between his thighs. A few times I felt his thighs squirming against my erect manhood between them.

"Somehow Patty boy I truly get the feeling that a very secret part of you loves this shit, its' what you've been waiting for," Vinny chided me. "That secret part of you being what I have of yours between my thighs at the moment..."

"FUCKER! I am not enjoying this shit! ARRRRRRRRR!" I railed and my head snapped up as he gave me ten, count them, ten hard fast swats in burning succession.

The sound of those ten swats so fast against my ass cheeks was enough to nearly drive me insane. The sensation was stinging and scaring buds.

"Like I told you my cock is always hard, and bein' that I got a hot date tonight on my mind makes me even more hard and drippy there," I prattled on stupidly. "Its thoughts of my lovely lady that got me all worked up in the cock, not you spanking the tar out of me like I was some misbehaved child. JEEZ!"

In response Vinny thwacked my ass hard with his paddle, getting some more loud screams out of me.

"You obviously forgot what I told you earlier Pat, your date tonight has been canceled, courtesy of me," Vinny said and swatted, swatted and swatted my ass (WHACK WHACK WHACK) hard till I was amazed to feel tears welling up in my eyes. "And seeing as your cock is always hard I'll tell you this, from now on if you don't pay your rent on time your ass will ALWAYS, ALWAYS be red. How's that sound Patty boy? Trust me on this ass-wipe, if your rent is not on time from here on out I'll come up there and get you just like I did tonight! Don't think that once my parents are back that they'll stop me from doing this! You will be spanked every time your rent is late! If not, like I said you can look elsewhere for lodgings!"

I clenched my teeth hard and tried my damndest to endure the awful searing pain as he tanned my behind, lecturing me at the same fucking time.

"GAWD, what the fuck'll I tell Linda?" I ranted through my clenched teeth and as Vinny spanked my ass I felt my tears start dripping down my face. "She'll think I stood her up, JEEZ!"

"Why don't you just tell her the truth ass wipe?" Vinny asked me in reply and swatted, SWATTED and swatted my ass harder and harder with his racquet ball paddle. "Tell her that you're a lazy excuse for a tenant who was late one time too many with his rent check and the landlord's son taught you a much deserved lesson?"

"OH YEAH, hardy fucking har, har," I grunted in between screaming in pain with each thrash of the paddle against my ass cheeks. "Like I just might tell her that...OWWWWW!"

After what felt like nearly one hundred swats to my poor ass cheeks with his goddamned hard plastic racquet ball paddle Vinny stood me up and hustled me quickly over to a workout horse, holding me tight by the back of my neck as I plodded along stupidly on my socked feet. The way he held me

56

so tightly by my neck forced me to simply look straight ahead. The spot on my face where he'd slapped me earlier felt like it was swelling up.

"Fucking bastard," I grunted, holding up my tied hands in front of me and desperately trying to free them, my cock swinging hard and erect in front of me like a goddamned flag on a pole, mortified to my core let me tell you.

As I walked toward the workout horse I could actually feel the cheeks of my ass twitching with redness...and with the sick realization that Vinny was far from done with me...

He proceeded to bend me over the workout horse on my stomach so that my arms dangled down in front of me, my sexy legs dangled behind me and my ass cheeks pointed straight up at heaven. GAWD! I squirmed miserably as the lame-brained stack of muscles squatted under the workout horse and bound my wrists to my ankles now.

"OH NO, NO, you fucker," I bantered as he tied me. "I need to be outa here and on my way to pick up Linda you madman! I waited so long for this date tonight!"

"Well then Patty boy, maybe this will teach you a lesson on paying your rent on time from now on," Vinny said as he got to his feet and ran a hand over my crimson and what felt like welted ass cheeks. "Consider this part three of your lessons here with me tonight."

"Get your mangy hands off me you degenerate!" I ranted as I hung on that fucking horse, feeling totally violated.

I nearly blanched when he wedged a finger into my hole and quickly extracted it.

"PERVERT!" I seethed.

Vinny chuckled and I managed to lift my head up enough to see him hanging his racquet ball paddle back on the wall hook from where he had gotten it. Looking around his gym I saw my underpants on the floor, GAWD!

To my horror of all horrors I saw Vinny next approaching me with a leather strop in hand; no doubt he used it for securing his wrists to workout apparatuses where he would have to chin-up or hoist himself when exercising. This time though the strop would be used to tan my poor ass some more.

"OH NO, no, come on Vinny, haven't you done enough to me buddy?" I cried out as he positioned himself beside me.

"Oh now I'm your buddy huh Patty boy?" he asked me. "You fucking ass wipe, never again will my father have to come knocking for your rent!"

He pushed me a tad further forward on the workout horse so that now he had both access to my ass cheeks and my under-thighs for spanking purposes. I involuntarily curled my bound hands around my socked ankles and I felt my cock emanate another dollop of pre-seed as I hung there like a side of beef.

Suddenly, WHACK WHACK WHACK WHACK WHACK came the awful and resounding noises of my ass cheeks being mightily stropped.

"AAAAAARRRHHHHHHH!" I wailed tremendously, my shrieks of pain bouncing off the gym/basement walls.

A few times in between whacking my ass cheeks with the strop Vinny deliberately swiped my under-thighs. That felt worse than my ass being stropped let me tell you. I felt my fear-hard cock swinging below me and every time he whacked my under-thighs my balls churned and seemed to cook up more sperm in them...

"EEEERRRRR!" I heard myself screaming through clenched teeth as my ass got redder and redder and as visions of Linda danced in my head.

I knew that by now I should have been on my way to pick her up for our date...oh woe is me! When Vinny had come to my door I had an hour and a half leeway time. By now it was most definitely too late, seeing as Vinny had for sure been spanking me for close to that amount of time. What a twisted turn of events took place that night huh?

Vinny pressed a huge hand against my lower back and then gave me what felt like upwards of twenty fast swipes in succession with his leather strop.

"OWWWWWWWW! VINNY, come on man, stop this already!" I ranted, begging at that point. "I-I've learned my lesson buddy! I'll always pay my rent on time!"

"I know that Patty boy, I'm just making sure now," Vinny laughed and proceeded to again swat at my under thighs, bringing wrenching sobs from deep within me and more tears streamed down my face. "As my dad taught me when I was growing up the first spanks are to teach you discipline and to make you realize your errors. The spanks following those are to reassure the man who spanked you that he did a good job and that you've learned your lesson."

WHACK WHACK WHACK WHACK WHACK sang Vinny's leather strop as it connected unforgivingly and searingly to my displayed ass cheeks. I whispered the words "Fucking bastard" over and over under my breath, swearing some kind of revenge on the dumb muscle head.

When Vinny stopped swatting my ass with his leather strop it felt like it was a holy mass of bruises and welts. After untying me and hauling me off the workout horse I stood there crying, hopping from foot to foot and rubbing my poor cheeks with the palms of my hands.

"You fucking bastard, you sick, sick excuse for a landlord," I blubbered, spittle flying from my mouth, tears streaming down my face and my lips quivering as I tried to speak coherently as Vinny hung his leather strop back up again. "YOU CAN'T HAVE DONE THIS TO ME MAN!"

Vinny turned and smiled smugly at me.

"Still need more?" he asked, holding up an open-palmed

hand.

Thoughts of him whaling into me with the back of his hand caused me to shut my yap real quickly! I backed away from him as fast as my socked feet would take me and bounded up the stairs two at a time, my ass cheeks smarting with every step I took. I heard Vinny snickering as I fumbled with the locked basement door trying to make my way out of that hell hole he had brought me down to.

"I'll expect the rent money first thing in the morning Patty boy," Vinny yelled up at me holding up the key to the door.

"Yes, yes," I stammered, looking down at him desperately, seeing that the degenerate weight-lifter had my underpants sticking out of his shorts pocket as he mocked me with the key to the basement door. "Let me the fuck out of here, please man..."

"Yes what Patty boy?" Vinny chided me as he approached the stairs, looking up at me.

"Yes Sir," I railed. "Yes Sir, yes Mr. Giordano, yes Daddy, just let me out of here!"

Vinny laughed hysterically, saw that he had achieved what he wanted and tossed me the key to freedom. I unlocked the door, pushed it open and tossed the key back down to the man I had just called "Daddy." I bolted from the basement, through his parent's house and up the stairs that led to my apartment.

I thanked God that I lived in a private house and that there were no other tenants to see me in my most embarrassing situation ever. Naked but for my dress socks I slammed my apartment door shut and stood there sniveling, still letting my tears flow... The fucking guy had kept my goddamned underpants like some kind of twisted souvenir of his conquest over me! JEEZ!

"FUCKING SHIT HEAD, fucking goddamned stupid stack

of muscles," I reeled, leaning against the door and not realizing it as I took my hard pulsing cock in hand and began slowly stroking it.

I pressed my reddened ass cheeks against the door and it cooled them slightly as I jacked myself off slowly...

"Bastard, spanked me like I was a little kid or something," I said softly, my tears still flowing as I looked at the clock and realized that it was too late to try to pick up Linda and still make our date.

HA! Even if I did go out on the date with Linda I wondered how the fuck I would be able sit comfortably either in a car or in a restaurant. I could just imagine the look on Linda's face if I asked our waiter to bring me a pillow to sit on, hardy fucking har, har! As I thought of Linda and as the pain from my reddened ass seared through my being I shot the mother of all loads all over my chest and stomach areas, grunting like a marine in heat as I seemed to cum and cum...my slop landed on me in thick gushes...

From outside my apartment door I swore that I heard the sound of Vinny's mocking laughter.

"Looks like I got me my own spank boy..." I heard Vinny say outside in the hallway.

Spanked by my Landlord's Son

(The Next Day)

Written by: Christopher Trevor

GAWD! I must be the only so and so in creation that was ever spanked by his landlord's son. I mean, how many guys out there are late with the rent from time to time? No big deal right? It happens to the best of us every once in a while. Okay, I had really overdone it with being late with the rent, I will admit to that. I suppose being that the landlord never really did anything about it I just kept on taking advantage. But I never expected to be spanked for it. The last six months I was late each month, six months right in a row. And I have to say that up until the fifth month Mr. Giordano, my old-world minded Italian landlord was pretty lenient with me. So when I was late the sixth month in a row with the rent I would have to say that my landlord had every right to be irate, but, BUT...to have been fucking spanked like a little kid because of it? And by the landlord's muscle-bound dopey son no less? JEEZ, but

I was pissed off. It wasn't even the landlord himself who had spanked me; it was his muscle stack of a son... JEEZ, I couldn't believe that I was actually weighing the differences between being spanked by the landlord himself or his village idiot of a son. Revenge and lawsuit were two words that kept popping into my brain the next morning...

These were the thoughts that were running rampant in my mind as I made my way to the bank in my neighborhood the following Saturday morning after the most embarrassing event of my life had taken place the night before. Not only was it beyond mortifying the way Vinny the muscle head had paraded me down to his basement/gym by my ear while I was clad in just my boxer briefs and silk office socks; but I also missed out on a date with the most beautiful woman I had ever met. Fucker, he took me by surprise by grabbing me by my goddamned ear, as if I was a misbehaved child or something thereof! FUCK and my ear was still smarting the next morning. I would make sure to mention that in my lawsuit as well, if I decided to serve the fucking asshole with one that is. When I called Linda (the pretty lady I was supposed to have gone out on a date with the night before) an hour after Vinny had done his dirty work tanning my behind till it was raw, red and welted there was no answer. I left her three messages, begging her forgiveness, telling her that I had gotten unexpectedly "tied up", which was actually kind of true, seeing as that meathead "HAD" tied me the fuck up while spanking me. GAWD! As I walked to the bank my poor butt cheeks still smarted. There was no way I could have driven there. Sitting down was still not an option. I could still feel the stinging redness as I strode down the avenue. Even the soft white cotton briefs I was wearing under my jeans weren't doing much to alleviate the horrid burning sensations. It was amazing I had slept at all the night before, what with the pain I was in. Damn that mutton brained asshole. What a sight I made standing in my bathroom last night, or, to be more precise, hopping around in my bathroom on my still socked feet while I rubbed fucking aloe cream on my wounded ass cheeks. The cream had soothed me a little but as soon as I sat down on the toilet to take a dump I realized just how little the cream had really soothed me at all.

It would more than likely be a couple of days before my ass cheeks were healed... I wondered how they would be feeling come Monday morning. Thoughts of sitting on a subway train's hard seat and then having to sit at my desk at my bank job all day were horrifying. I was thinking I would probably have to call in sick. Can you imagine having to take a fucking sick day because your ass cheeks are too wounded to sit down on? JEEZ!

And not only had the stupid fucker spanked me till my ass shined as red as a fire engine but he had also kept the damned underpants I had been wearing when he'd come to my apartment door. What the fuck kind of sleaze-bag does that I ask you? Fucking guy had taken my damned under shorts off me to really get at reddening my poor hiny, FUCK, fuck and double fucks! Thoughts of him sniffing my damned underpants and jacking off filled my mind. I couldn't really judge the guy on that though, seeing as for whatever the fuck the reason after Vinny had let me go back up to my apartment I had jacked off like never before in my life. Somehow the mixture of the pain of my tanned behind and thoughts of Linda, my ill fated date combined made me hornier than a minx. I couldn't figure it out only that it was the most intense explosion I had ever had in all my young life.

When I got to the bank at eight-thirty AM I walked up to one of the three ATM machines. I prayed that I had money in my checking account to cover the month's rent. If not I was sure I could look forward to another ass tanning at the hands of Vinny the muscle head. FUCK! What a thing for a grown guy to be dreading. Little did I know at that moment what was in store for me that day though... I'll simply say this for the moment, Vinny the muscle head was far from done with yours truly here.

After inserting my ATM card into the machine I inputted my pin number. I pressed "withdrawal" to access money from my checking account and when the words "insufficient funds" lit up on the screen I nearly shit my pants.

"FUCK!" I ranted and punched the wall.

I could already feel my ass cheeks stinging anew. Shit, if I didn't get that rent money I knew that Vinny would spank me again...and this time he would be even more severe than the night before. Somehow I just knew that, my ass cheeks told me so. The machine slid my card back out to me and I quickly inserted it again, figuring I would just have to dip into my savings account to get the money. As I re-input my pin number I thanked God that I had thought not to give Vinny a check that morning when I saw him working out (as usual) in the backyard of the house. Fucking guy was so scantily clad in a pair of posing trunks and sneakers with no socks that it amazed me he wasn't arrested for exposing himself. Had I given him a check it would have no doubt bounced, no, better to just give the sawed off muscle head cold hard cash. As I had left the house I had waved over to him as he hefted what looked like thousands of pounds worth of weight on a bar as he lay on a bench. I had all to do to go over there and kick him in the balls for what he had done to me the night before. Instead of smiling back at me in greeting Vinny simply smirked. I supposed he was smirking at the fact that I was walking sort of funny. After I input my pin number and punched the withdrawal button for savings I was told that I had already exceeded the amount of money that I could withdraw during the last twenty-four hours.

"FUCK AGAIN!" I snarled as I retrieved my ATM card a second time, remembering how I had taken money out the day before to purchase a new button down shirt and tie for the date I was going to go on the night before, the date that never happened. "GOD DAMN it all!"

As my ass cheeks were twitching another guy came in and used the ATM machine next to the one I was using. When he withdrew what looked like nearly a thousand fucking dollars and walked away with it I could have cried. Okay, I had to think. I could take a cash advance with my credit card. It was my last hope. Well, that or beg my parents for some money, but after having moved out of my parents house on not such good terms I didn't think they would be too keen on having to foot my rent for me. With my hands shaking

I put my ATM card back in my wallet and took out my Visa credit card. I inserted it into the slot and for the third time that morning punched the button marked "withdrawal" after inputting my pin number. When the machine asked me how much I would like to withdraw I breathed a sigh of relief that I was sure could have been heard way down the block. With my hand trembling I inputted the amount I wanted to withdraw. I could not believe the effect Vinny the muscle head had had on me, to the point that my hands were shaking while using a goddamned ATM machine. As the money came out of the machine I could have cried tears of joy. Fuck, it's better than the tears of pain and outright humiliation I had cried the night before that's for sure. I quickly tucked the money in my pocket, retrieved my ATM card and started back to the house. I figured I would give Vinny the bodybuilding dork his money and make him write me out a receipt. Seeing as I would be handing over a huge wad of cash it made sense to get a receipt. After that I would try again to get Linda on the phone. Maybe she and I could re-schedule our failed date from the night before for the following weekend. No way could I see her tonight, seeing as it would be pretty humiliating to ask for a pillow to sit on in a restaurant if she and I decided to go out for dinner. With the money in my pocket I felt much better about things...well; at least I would for a short while.

When I got to the house I made my way quickly to the backyard figuring I would give Vinny the cash then and there. I had no problem whatsoever interrupting the guy while he was working out. No problem at all right? RIGHT! Actually, he deserved to be interrupted; he deserved that and more after what he had done to me the night before. Every time I thought about it my damned ass cheeks twitched and my cock churned in my pants. What was up with that I ask you? I fleetingly remembered hearing him outside the door to my apartment after he'd listened to me jacking off, saying that he now had his own spank boy. I shuddered at the very thought of that.

In the backyard I saw Vinny's weight bench and his weights scattered around it but there was no sign of him anywhere. I guessed he was in the house, more than likely

67

now working out in his basement/gym, the scene of the crime from last night. As I thought about it again I rubbed my ear. I sauntered up to the front door of the house and rang the doorbell.

"It's open, come on in Brego!" I heard Vinny's deep voice call out from inside the house.

I stupidly ignored a feeling of foreboding that engulfed me for a moment and stepped into the house, my hand in my pocket, reaching for the cash at the same time.

"I have your money Vinny," I said as I stepped into the main dining room of the house, looking around for the Herculean landlord's son. "Vinny?"

I didn't see him anywhere as I slowly made my way through the dining room, which led off to the living room. The house was beautifully decorated I have to say. Oak furniture filled the living room and like most Italian families they had a huge mirror placed over the couch. All the walls were painted creamy white, jeez!

"Vinny?" I called out again, the wad of money now clutched tightly in my fist as I searched for the dorky muscle bound frump.

It felt sort of weird to be prowling around inside my landlord's house looking for the landlord's son, the landlord's son who the night before had tanned my ass cheeks to the color of a fire engine. My cock churned in my pants and for whatever the fuck the reason I could feel my balls shifting in their sac.

"Yo Vinny, I'm here with your money!" I called loudly.

Once again I figured he was in the basement and I started making my way in that direction. As I walked further through the house toward the basement steps entrance memories of the night before and being forced down here by my ear wreaked havoc on me. Shit, I could actually feel my poor ear twitching as I walked slowly toward the basement.

"Vinny? Mr. Giordano?" I called out, now feeling very uncertain about this whole set-up.

Suddenly that's how I was feeling, set up.

"Are you down there Vinny?" I called out, standing a few feet away from the basement stairs, tucking the money back into my jeans pocket. "Vinny, Sir?"

"Right here ass wipe," I heard from behind me and quickly whirled around.

Standing there in his royal blue posing trunks and sneakers the muscle head made a most imposing muscular figure, totally filling the space where I would have to walk to get back upstairs to my apartment.

"I uh, I got your money Vinny, uh, Mr. Giordano," I said, patting the front right sided pocket of my jeans.

"Hmm, last night it was "Daddy", now its Vinny and Mr. Giordano again huh Patty boy?" he asked me, sounding totally sadistic. "Huh ass wipe?"

"Look man, I just want to forget about last night okay?" I asked him, trembling in my mustard colored work boots as I stood there before him, not wanting to, but taking in the sight of his jutted up fat nipples on his huge chest. "I just want to pay my rent and move on."

"Just move on Patty boy?" he asked me, repeating my words. "What about all the months before when you were late? Should my father just move on from that? You think he'll just forget the aggravation you caused him?"

As the guy spoke he was slowly coming toward me, stepping inch by inch...

"Look Vinny, I mean Mr. Giordano," I began.

"It's Daddy ass wipe, from now on for you I'm *Daddy*," he seethed at me through clenched teeth, the huge bowling ball sized biceps in his upper arms seeming to be flexing and twitching involuntarily.

I quickly saw that his cock was semi erect in his posing trunks and I swear I saw a tiny stain of pre seed on the front of them. Hearing him say that from now on he was "Daddy" to me infuriated me.

"Now look man, what you and I have here is a business relationship," I said, making the mistake of holding up a hand and pointing a finger at the mountain of muscles. "I'm willing to forget about what happened last night but "Daddy" is totally out of..."

Suddenly, with lightning like speed Vinny reached forward and grabbed my wrist in a Vise-like death grip.

"AAAWWWWRRRRR!" I wailed at the sudden pain as he hefted me forward, nearly lifting me out of my damned boots. "OWWWWWWWW!"

As he squeezed my wrist he turned his hand slowly against it, giving me what when we were kids we used to call an "Indian burn."

"AAAARRRR! SHIT, let go of me man!" I bantered angrily in his face.

As I clenched my other hand into a fist, ready to pummel the guy, if that was possible, Vinny quickly spun me around facing forward, bringing my arm behind me as he held onto it tightly at the wrist.

"OOWWWWWW SHHHIIITTTT!" I railed as my arm was twisted up behind me and I now faced the basement stairs, memories of the previous night flooding my brain. "Vinny, you bastard, this hurts, you're gonna break my goddamned arm!"

"Move it Patty boy, you have your second appointment with me down in my home gym right now!" Vinny said directly into my ear from behind me, his lips grazing my ear as he spoke, and his crotch up against my backside.

He began moving me toward the stairs, holding my arm

up behind me, the pain awful.

"VINNY, no, NO!" I pleaded. "NOT THIS AGAIN MAN! I got you your rent money, I told you!"

"Later for that ass wipe, you still need to learn a lesson for the last six months you were late with the rent..." he said, slowly moving me down the stairs and into his basement/gym.

"Fuck your lesson; you can't do this to me!" I ranted and he pushed me forward, nearly toppling me off balance and almost careening me down the stairs. "YOWWWWWW!"

I started reeling off words like lawsuit, lawyer, and how I would take his muscle bound ass to court. Vinny simply chuckled behind me, told me I was welcome to try those things and said how it would all be his word against mine.

"OH YEAH you muscle dork?" I asked him. "And what about my poor reddened behind? Would that be my word against yours?"

As I asked him that we reached the bottom of the stairs and Vinny hustled me over to the same rubber floor mat from the night before. Images of me showing my reddened ass cheeks to judge in a courtroom flitted through my mind and I realized how humiliating that would be. Vinny flung me bodily and I went hobbling forward and landed flat on my ass on the mat, uttering the sound of "OOOFFF" as I plopped down.

"Damn it man!" I grunted.

As I slowly got myself to my feet, the pain in my arm immense Vinny sauntered over to a thigh-press machine and picked up a thin leather belt that had been placed on the seat of the workout device. With my left hand I massaged the area of my right arm where Vinny had twisted it so badly. Holding the leather belt in hand Vinny took a few steps toward me and said, "Strip down to your underpants and socks Patty boy!"

My face grimaced into a look of utter disbelief at what I

71

had just heard him say. Was he kidding?

"Thanks anyway Vinny, but I really don't feel like lifting weights and working out with you down here in your homemade gym," I said snidely.

Suddenly, the oversized muscle guy swung the thin leather belt and it connected painfully with my left upper arm, the sound a swiping and stinging "WHACCCK" filling the air.

"OWWWWW!" I roared. "You son of a bitch!"

I angrily clenched my hands into fists, ready to do battle with him, forgetting the fact that he outweighed, out-towered and out-muscled me by what must have been at least hundreds of sheer muscular pounds.

"I'll teach you to spank a paying tenant," I said as I approached him.

He chuckled as if I had just said the stupidest thing and when I was close enough to him he swatted a huge hand against my chest, sending me spiraling backward.

"HUUNNFFFF!" I gasped as I toppled back to the rubber mat, landing again flat on my backside.

I realized that I was dealing with more than I could handle here. FUCK! What a predicament I was in...the soft brained hard muscled asshole was going to spank me again and it looked like this time I was in for it with a rather old looking leather belt.

"Strip down to your underpants and socks ass wipe and if I have to say it a third time you're going to be sorrier than you already are," Vinny said sternly, stepping over to me and looming menacingly over me as I lay there on the mat.

Looking up at him I saw the outline of his big balls in his skimpy posing trunks. My cock churned at the sight and scent of that. I still could not get my arms around that line of thinking, FUCK!

The belt that he was no doubt going to use to spank me with dangled at his side...

Whimpering miserably I sat up on my ass on the mat and with my fingers trembling began unlacing my work boots.

"No expensive suit and tie today eh Patty boy?" Vinny asked me, stepping away from me as I shucked off my boots, revealing my white sweat socked feet.

"It's Saturday man, I don't work on Saturdays!" I replied, getting to my feet and pulling my pull-over shirt off.

"Let me tell you about this belt Patty boy," Vinny said as I slowly stripped down to my underpants and sweat socks. "It belonged to my grandfather. Whenever my dad misbehaved when he was a kid and even sometimes when he was as old as in his twenties this was the belt my grandfather used on him to teach him a lesson. When I was growing up my grandfather passed the belt to my dad and he used it on me whenever discipline was called for. Now the belt is mine. And when I have kids somewhere down the line it will be used to discipline them when needed."

"What a fucked up heirloom," I said softly as I unhitched my belt while standing there shirtless in front of my landlord's son.

"You should feel honored that this belt is going to be used right now to redden your ass cheeks some more ass wipe," Vinny said, folded the belt in two and made a snapping sound with it.

I flinched at that sound and also at the sound of him continually calling me "ass wipe." With my jeans off now and in hand I said, "Fucker, you have no right to be doing this to me. I brought you your damned money..." and slammed my jeans down on the floor. As Vinny smiled mockingly at me I stood on the rubber mat before him clad now in just my white Calvin Klein tight fitting briefs and white calf length sweat socks. My cock was fear hard and outlined erotically in my briefs, my sweaty balls churning in there as well.

73

"I'll take your money later Patty boy, after I'm done teaching you a lesson," Vinny said, his voice totally filled with authority. "Now, let me show you how my thigh press machine works. GET OVER HERE, NOW!"

He swung the belt through the air and it made a whooshing sound as he and I stepped over to his thigh press exercise device... My heart thundered in my chest...

We stood on either side of the thigh press machine, me with my hands clasped behind me per Vinny's asinine orders. Given the size, strength and girth of the guy I felt it best to do as I was told, much as I would regret that.

"This machine is used to build up and strengthen the backs of the thighs," Vinny said, explaining his machine as if he was a personal trainer and I was his client. "You lay on the seat with your stomach area completely over said seat. In that position your ass is pointed directly upwards."

As he spoke he leered at me manically and I took a deep breath of total trepidation. The fact that he said "my ass" would be pointing directly upwards made me feel not so great about my current situation...

"Now Patty boy, you can look at today's session as another lesson that I'm teaching you when it comes to paying your rent on time," Vinny said and pointed at me and then at the cushioned seat of his backs of the thighs exercise machine.

"Is that what all this is going to come to be called, my sessions?" I asked him, sounding bitter as all hell.

"You can see it however the fuck you want ass wipe, as far as I'm concerned you brought all this on yourself," Vinny said and again pointed at the seat of the machine, this time with a look of fierce determination in his eyes.

I swallowed a gulp of fear and did as I was told. I lay down on the machine with my stomach directly over the seat. The guy had been right. In this position my ass pointed straight up, a perfect and ready target for his damned heirloom/belt.

From behind me Vinny positioned my sweat socked feet under the roller connected to the weights. He then squatted in front of me and to my mounting horror tied my wrists off to the handles in front of me.

"For the first round of spanking you today I'll give you a break Patty boy," Vinny laughed as he tied my wrists to the machine handles, his face dangerously close to mine as he spoke.

"Yeah, what kind of break?" I asked him miserably.

"I'll leave your underpants on you for round one," he snickered and I looked at him angrily. "After that it's off come the undies and your ass gets a good old-fashioned tanning."

"You fucking crazy guy, my ass is still red from last night," I pouted as Vinny finished lashing my wrists to the machine handles.

"Your ass is going to be red from now on, remember, from here on out you're my own personal spank boy ass wipe. You should be grateful that I've taken such an interest in you and your well being..." Vinny said sounding campy as hell as he gave my nose a squeeze and to my shock kissed my cheek before standing up beside me, taking his heirloom/belt in hand.

"Vinny, I'll tell your parents about this!" I yelled out, thinking that was my final hope.

Perhaps with that threat he would untie me and let me go...but no such luck...as he brought the damned folded up belt down hard on my upturned briefs clad ass cheeks.

SWATTT SWATTT SWATTT SWATTT SWATTT

"OWWWW, holy shit!" I screamed the pain immense seeing as my poor ass cheeks had suffered similar treatment less than twenty-four hours ago.

"Tell my parents?" he asked me, sounding totally mocking. "And just what do you think they'll do to me when

I tell them that because I made you into my spank boy that from now on you're going to pay the rent on time?"

SWATTT SWATTT SWATTT SWATTT SWATTT

"OHHHRRRR, FUCKER!" I ranted up at him, my head slightly turned so I was able to watch as he swung the damned belt.

It stung like the devil as he reddened my already red ass cheeks. I could feel new welts bubbling up already on the wounded skin. It seemed that every muscle in his huge arms and broad shoulders were flexing as he flung the belt back and brought it fast and hard back down against my ass cheeks.

SWATTT SWATTT SWATTT SWATTT SWATTT

"The way I see it Patty boy my parents will thank me for having taken over making sure that their delinquent tenant pays his rent on time," Vinny said and swatted me again and again, harder with each blow it seemed.

"OH yeah? You overgrown kid," I seethed as tears formed in my eyes. "When I move the fuck out of here we'll see if the next tenant you get in this dump puts up with shit like this!"

SWATTT SWATTT SWATTT SWATTT SWATTT

"Like I told you last time I spanked you ass wipe, with the cheap ass rent you pay here I don't see you moving out any time soon," the muscle bound idiot said and swatted, swatted and swatted my ass again and again with his heirloom/belt.

"AAAAARHHHHHHHHH!" I cried out in anguish.

"We'll see if I don't move the hell out of here Vinny, Mr. Giordano!" I screamed at him, facing forward again and taking in the awful sight of my bound wrists. "NO way I'll stay here and pay to be anyone's goddamned spank boy... AAAARRRRRRHHHH!"

SWATTT SWATTT SWATTT SWATTT SWATTT

"I guess we'll just see about that now won't we Patty boy?" he teased me as he thrashed my ass over and over, him breathing heavily now as he swatted me over and over. "I mean, lets face it, you're here now again after what I did to you last night."

"And just what in fucking fucks is that supposed to mean muscle head?" I grunted as he swatted my ass. "AAARRHHHHHHHH!"

"It means, ass wipe, that most guys would not have come anywhere near me after having suffered what I did to you already," Vinny said. "But today you walked right into my clutches. Face it ass wipe, you want to be my spank boy...."

SWATTT SWATTT SWATTT SWATTT SWATTT

"NO, no, that's not it at all!" I sobbed, tears streaming down my face at this point. "I just came to pay my rent, that's all, THAT's all Vinny, Mr. Giordano...*D-daddy...*"

Vinny's face lit up in a smile from ear to ear at the sound of my having called him "Daddy" yet again...

After giving me what must have been upwards of nearly one hundred swats on my briefs covered ass with his heirloom/ belt the mutton-headed muscle guy stopped his romp. He hung his belt on the exercise device beside the one I was tethered to.

"Okay Patty boy, I'll let you rest for about five minutes while I get your briefs off you and tend to this red welted ass of yours," Vinny said, slid my socked feet out from under the weight rollers letting my legs dangle and slowly peeled my briefs off me.

As he unveiled my poor reddened ass the cool air against it felt weird somehow. I was sniveling and crying like a baby, my tears dripping from my eyes and landing on the matted gym floor.

"FUCKER, bastard," I shrieked as I felt my balls dangling

77

under me, chock filled yet again with my manly juices.

Embarrassing as all hell my cock was betraying me again by being harder than a goddamned diamond.

"Damn, your ass is really crimson Patty boy, real cherry looking," Vinny teased me, running the palm of his hand over my ass cheeks.

He meanly squeezed a couple of the welts that had formed back there as well, getting a few loud shrieks of man's anguish out of me. I huffed and blubbered, muttering the words "thank you" over and over as he rubbed some aloe cream over my much wounded ass cheeks.

"This will keep you from bleeding during the next round of spanking to come ass wipe," Vinny said and had I not been tied to that device I would have flown off it as he slid a thick finger into my shit chute and prodded it around in there.

"PLEASE VINNY, please, *please, no more for today,*" I cried out desperately. "You know by now that I'll pay my goddamned rent on time! You know I'll be respectful! Man, you know I'll call you "Daddy."

"Oh yes, I know all that and much more Patty boy," Vinny chuckled, sounding like a proud parent. "But now we're at a point where I have to be sure that my lessons have sunk in. That's how my dad did it with me. You see, I know you could be saying those things thinking that I'll untie you and let you go. I know I would be saying anything to get out of the position you're presently in. I remember all too well myself..."

As he spoke my cock churned under me and I swore to him that I was telling the truth, begging him at that point not to spank me anymore...

But alas, he simply put the aloe cream aside, slid my sweat socked feet back under the weight rollers and once more picked up his heirloom/belt.

"OH GAWD," I muttered and saw my discarded briefs

hanging down the side of his posing trunks, also noting how his cock was rock hard in those damned skimpy trunks of his.

Fuck, I stupidly thought how that would be two pairs of my underpants that this overgrown muscle head had scored from me. I realized that going forward I would have to come wearing no underpants when I brought Vinny the rent. I could not believe that those were the thoughts racing through my head as he took up position again next to me. He raised his heirloom/belt and...***SWATTT SWATTT SWATTT SWATTED*** my now naked and creamed up ass cheeks...

"AAAYYYRRRRRRR DADDY please no more!" I yelped loudly, swearing to myself that somehow, SOMEHOW I would get even with this miserable bastard.

Each time his heirloom/belt connected with my tenderized ass cheeks I thought for sure I was going to start bleeding back there. But Vinny knew what he was doing when he had creamed up my cheeks. The blows now hurt even more but at the same time I would not bleed. How about that huh buds?

SWATTT SWATTT SWATTT SWATTT SWATTT

"ARRRHHHHHHHHHH!" I ranted through a now very scratchy throat.

I wondered just how much longer he planned on keeping me down in his home gym that day. I also wondered when the hell his parents would be coming back from their trip. Wait till I tell those two off the boat ignoramuses what their jock head son had done to me I thought, figuring I would also tell them that I was planning on suing him and their sorry asses...

SWATTT SWATTT SWATTT SWATTT SWATTT

After a while all I heard and felt was the sound of the belt as it connected with my red, red ass cheeks. I cried loudly and begged my "Daddy" to stop swatting me. It seemed to me however that my cries of anguish only spurred him on all the more...

When he finally did stop swatting my ass we were both sweating like mad, for different reasons obviously.

"Okay Patty boy, seeing as your ass was already red I'll let you go with just two rounds of spanking for today," Vinny said and from my tied down position I watched him hang his heirloom/belt on a wall hook.

He turned and took in the sight of me as I lay there crying like a fucking baby...

A few minutes later I was untied from the exercise device and dressed...minus my underpants of course. It seemed that each time Vinny spanked me he planned to keep my damned underpants. As I handed him the rent money, still crying mind you he told me to stock up on underpants, seeing as he could decide to spank me at any given moment. I could not believe what I was hearing it as I stood there handing him the rent money...

"Okay ass wipe, you're done with today's session," Vinny said to me, giving me a quick open handed friendly sort of slap on the ass.

Being that I was wearing jeans softened the blow a bit, but at the same time, being that my ass cheeks were red as beets it still smarted. My cock throbbed as I free-balled in my jeans.

"Th-thank you Mr. Giordano, Daddy, Sir," I mumbled as I headed for the stairs.

From behind me Vinny laughed meanly and I slowly made my way upstairs to my apartment...

Once in my apartment I quickly stripped out of my clothes, threw every tray of ice cubes I had in my freezer into the bathtub and sat with my poor wounded ass cheeks on ice as I jacked off for the second time after having been spanked to within an inch of my life...

"Fucking bastard, fucking muscle bound asshole," I

swore as I held my hard cock tight and slowly stroked myself to yet another amazing gusher...the likes of which I seemed to be able to achieve only after having been spanked by my landlord's son...

Dad's Discipline

Written by: Eddie Knapps

In the house where I grew up, my Dad believed there were only two punishments a boy understood.

One was getting his driver's license taken away. The other was getting a spanking.

If you didn't have a license then there was only one other alternative.

Dad grew up in West Virginia, and there, back then, bare assed discipline was the rule. We were living in California in the seventies, but he said that what had been good enough for him when he was a kid was good enough for me and my two brothers. It got to be pretty embarrassing as we got older. Nobody else we knew was getting his teenaged butt warmed. Every few weeks, one of us would show up in gym with a bright red fanny, and all the guys would know exactly what had happened. Once, I'd gotten a real hard spanking for backtalk. One thing Dad would not abide is any of us being what he called "sassy." The next day I was drying off after my shower and one of the coaches walked through and saw me and shouted, "What in hell happened to that butt of yours, son?" Well, anybody who hadn't taken a gander at my ass sure did then. I was really embarrassed and kind of looked at the ground and said, "My Dad spanked me yesterday." The coach laughed and said, "I'll say he did! Probably just what you needed, huh? Ha!"

My two brothers—Larry and Frank—and I all got it, frequently, up to the time we could drive. It was always the same. Dad would call us back to the bedroom. He'd stand there frowning with his arms crossed and look at each one of us hard while we looked at the floor.

Then he'd say, "I think you need your bottom blistered!"

It wasn't that Dad was being coy or something. He'd wake us up in the morning by shouting, "Get those butts in gear up there!" Or he'd say to us, "Okay, you can go to the movies. But I want your little asses back here in time for supper." It was only when we got spanked that we had "bottoms," which was a word we learned to dread.

After he'd announced what was going to happen, Dad would stomp over to his bureau and get his hairbrush. It was a big, flat-faced, oval, wooden one, with a long handle on it that gave him plenty of leverage. It was about a quarter of an inch thick and made out of hardwood. I know people who think getting it with a hairbrush is sort of sissy or something. They obviously never got licked with one! The sting of that thing on your fanny was enough to send you into orbit.

After he got the brush, he'd sit down on his desk chair and order us over next to him. One by one, he'd open our flies, take us across his knee, and pull down our pants. We were never allowed to "let" our pants down. Dad didn't believe in that. He'd give a good yank and, all of a sudden, there you were, bent over and bare-bottomed. Then he'd start in with that brush.

Dad didn't believe he'd gotten through to you till you started to cry.

He said that was the time a boy really listened. Of course, just because you were bawling didn't mean the spanking stopped. If anything, Dad whacked our bottoms harder after the tears started, shouting out his lecture over the sound of our wailing and the whacking of the brush—"I'll teach you to...!" or "You think you're old enough to...! or "If I ever hear about you...!"

Of all of us, I think my oldest brother, Larry, got it the most. There was about two weeks once where he must've gotten spanked ten times. Frank probably got spanked the least—he was sort of serious and real well-behaved. I fell someplace in the middle. Larry was four years older than me, and Frank was three, so there came a time, after they got their licenses, when I was the only one who was still getting my bottom blistered. Dad actually kind of let up. In those years, there were probably a lot of times when I deserved to get spanked and didn't. But I still remember that last time when I was a boy. As a kid, that was probably the hardest and most embarrassing blistering I ever got.

I was actually already eighteen. My schedule at school had gotten screwed up, so I wasn't able to get into driver's education till my junior year. Then, I'd flunked my driving test twice. Maybe, too, it was that driving didn't make that much of a difference to me right then. I didn't have a car and I wasn't that much into dating. I'd double date with Frank if necessary, but mostly, I ran with a crowd of people, and there was always transportation, so why sweat it? I had my learner's permit, and I figured I'd get around to time three on the test sometime soon. Boy, did I regret not having gotten that matter settled sooner! A week before my next test was scheduled, as luck would have it, our report cards arrived.

Dad always demanded we keep at least a B average.

Larry was at the community college, and just squeaking by, and Frank was struggling at State. I was doing okay really, but I'd kind of sloughed off in the last weeks of the term because of water polo practice. I'd managed to maintain a C+, but that wasn't good enough for Dad.

He let a couple days go by without saying anything. I think all three of us thought maybe we'd gotten away with something. Then, on Saturday, Mom had gone off to do the shopping and we boys were sitting around watching a ball game. Dad came into the den and said: "All right. I want to see the lot of you back in the bedroom. Now!"

We knew what was up. We got up and went back to the bedroom and stood there in a row. Dad was sitting in his desk chair, and he gave us a good dressing down for not keeping our grades up. By the end of it, both Larry and Frank had their driver's licenses out of their pockets and I pulled out my learner's permit.

Dad went down the line, growling—"We'll see how you like taking the bus for a while," to Larry and "It's about time you got some exercise, lard ass" to

Frank. He was always riding Frank because he was a little overweight and not real athletic. Even though I was younger, I was already physically bigger than he was, and a lot stronger.

When Dad got to me, he looked at my hand and said, "What the hell is that?"

"My learner's permit," I said.

He got this real hard smile on his face. "You're getting a little big for your britches, aren't you, Mr. Water Polo? Turning into a real smarty-pants. The deal is that you lose your driver's license, and that's no driver's license you've got there. I think I know what you need. It's about time you got your bottom blistered!"

Both my brothers got these little smirks, and they told

86

me later I got an expression on my face like I'd just lost my last friend. Dad went over and got his hairbrush, and then planted himself on his chair.

"No, Dad," I squeaked.

My brothers' grins grew wider. They were going to see me get a licking without having gotten one themselves. Suddenly I realized that, as far as Dad was concerned, they were grown-ups and I wasn't. "Please!" I said again, pathetically.

Dad looked at me viciously. "Are you sassing me, boy?"

"No, sir," I said quickly. "No, sir."

"Well, then, I'll tell you something. If you're not over my knee in ten seconds, I'll make you do it. And if I have to do that, you're gonna regret it even more than you're gonna regret stalling now."

What could I do? I walked over and stood beside him, and felt Dad's hand roughly pull my pants open. He grabbed me by the arm and hauled me across his knee. Frank let out a little giggle, the fucker. Then, Dad's fingers pushed down beneath the waistband of my jeans and shorts, and, shoosh, they were both down there below my knees.

So, there I was—eighteen years old, bare assed, bent-over Dad's knee, my nose inches from the floor, right in front of my two older brothers.

TWACK!

"Ow!"

TWACK!

"Ouch!"

"Okay, smart aleck!" Dad said. TWACK! "Even if your brothers are too old to spank," TWACK! "you're not!" TWACK! "Your goddamn learner's permit!" TWACK! "Just who do you think you are?" TWACK!

"Ow! Ouch! Please, Dad! Ow! No!"

Jesus, it hurt! Dad never went after us light. From the very first, he really gave our bottoms a whaling. And this was all the worse from Larry and Frank being there. They just stood there and watched, and Larry told me later his own butt was just squirming real quietly, remembering what it had been like.

TWACK! TWACK! TWACK! TWACK!

"Owww! Nooo! Please, Dad! OWWW!"

When Dad said blistered, he meant blistered. He always said God gave boys a bottom so there'd be a place to spank. And, oh Lordy, did he know how to take a rear end out for a spin!

TWACK! TWACK!

"OWWWW! OWWWW!"

That hairbrush was merciless! Each whack of its hard thinness felt like a thousand pins pressed into my defenseless ass flesh. The sting of it was enough to get my rear end bucking lustily after only the first few spanks. And Dad was just warming up!

TWACK! "OWWWW!" TWACK! "YEE-OUCH!" TWACK! "AHHHH!"

He laid into my fanny like there was no tomorrow. It didn't take two minutes before my legs were kicking my pants down around my shoes.

TWACK! TWACK!

"OWWWW! OWWWW!"

And two minutes after that, I was bawling like a four year old.

"OWWW! NOOO! OWWW! WHAAAHH! WHAAAHHH!"

"TWACK! TWACK! TWACK!"

"OUCH! AHHHH! PLEEASSSEE! PLEASE, DAD! I'll do better! WHHAAAHH!

WHHAAAAHHH!""

"You goddamn will do better, you lazy little bastard!" TWACK! TWACK!

TWACK! "I'll teach you to get bad marks!" TWACK! TWACK! TWACK! "Think you're all grown up already, do you?" TWACK! TWACK! "You sassy little so-and-so!" TWACK! "You're goddamn learner's permit!" TWACK! "I'll show you, you little screw off!" TWACK!

TWACK! TWACK!

"WAAAH—HHAAHHH-AAAHHHH! WWAAHHAAAHHH..."

My legs were going like a windmill, my pants and underpants bunched down around my ankles and flying in the air like a flag. Frank says I was squirming so much he thought that I was going to fall off Dad's knee. I sure didn't have a shred of dignity left. I wiggled desperately from side to side, my cock and balls flapping around, and poking my rear end up in the air so my brothers got as good a look as they ever wanted at that teenage pucker of mine, all the while squalling like a five year old and pleading with Dad to stop. He sure had me where he wanted me, and I was getting a lesson I'd never forget. Larry told me he didn't think Dad had ever spanked him as hard as he spanked me that Saturday. I don't know what got into him. Maybe it was the grades, but I think more than that he was really pissed that I'd tried to wiggle out of my punishment. He just didn't let up.

TWACK! TWACK! TWACK! TWACK!

"OWWWW! NOOO! WHAAAHHH! DAD! I'll do better. OWWW! I will! OWWW!

OWWW! WHAAHH-AH-HAH-AH-HAHHHH!"

TWACK! TWACK! TWACK!

"WHHAA-HAAA-HAAHAAHAAA! WHAAAHAAAAAAAA!..."

TWACK! TWACK! TWACK! TWACK...

When it was finally over, I was crying like I hadn't cried in years, and

Frank and Larry sure weren't smirking anymore. I think they'd been a little freaked out at how badly Dad had blistered my bottom. It was red as a ripe tomato, with blisters all across it and from the top of my buns to my thighs.

He pushed me up off his lap. At first, I just lay there squalling with my nose to the floor and my fiery fanny spread open in the air.

"Get the hell up!" Dad yelled.

Once on my feet, I started rubbing my burning butt, still bawling to the air.

Beat of the band, standing there doing a little two step with my pants around my ankles in front of Dad and Larry and Frank, dancing up and down clawing at my throbbing rear while my furry cock and balls waved in the breeze. From all the stimulation down there, my pecker was half hard, but I didn't care. I couldn't even think about being embarrassed. The only thing I could concentrate on right then was somehow cooling the fire Dad had lit on my eighteen year old bottom.

"You get back to your room and you stay there till I come to get you out. And if you don't cut out that crying, I'll really give you something to cry about! Understand! Now, get going!"

I didn't even bother to pull my pants up. I just sort of shifted them above my knees and waddled my little red rear out of there. Frank and Larry weren't far behind either. We all spent the next twenty-four hours in our rooms.

You can bet I got my license the next week, and I suppose you'd figure that one was the last spankings I ever got. But it didn't quite work out that way...

Return to Dad's Discipline

Written by: Eddie Knapps

There I was—twenty-six years old—and something just wasn't right.

Somehow, I wasn't feeling good about myself. I was getting work done; my sex life was okay; I'd just bought myself a little house I was fixing up.

But I knew that there was something missing.

Part of it, I was sure, was that—even though the consulting I was doing was going all right—I really wasn't putting my all into it. And a lot of times, on weekends, when I'd have a project in mind—repairing the roof on the porch or getting those bookshelves installed in that hall—I'd just end up stretched out on the sofa, looking through a porno mag, having myself a noontime scotch, wanking my dick. My girlfriend at the time had broken up with me the previous month. Even she had said to me: "You know, Brett, I don't know what it is that's missing in your life, but I think you better think it about it. You're just not happy, and you need to figure out why!"

I did know what the root of the problem was, or at least, I thought I did. Somehow, I just didn't have enough self-discipline. I'd even taken some of those courses—you know the kinds that are supposed to teach you how to get your life in shape. But they just didn't work for me. After the last one, I'd gone out for a drink with one of the other guys in the class, and both of us agreed it really didn't convince us.

"You know," I said to him, "Sometimes I think all guys like us need is a good spanking now and then."

We'd both laughed about it. It was a pretty silly idea, after all.

Still, it hadn't been all that long since I'd gotten my pants pulled down.

My Dad had hair brushed me and my brothers, Frank and Larry, the whole time we were growing up. Hell, I got my last fanny-tanning at eighteen! I hadn't kept my grades up, and my old man had really taken it out of my hide, right there in front of twenty-three year old Frank and twenty-one year old Larry.

Boy, did he whale the tar out of me! And you can bet my grades improved.

So, sometimes, when I was thinking about how my life was going, I'd wonder if, even now, a dose of Dad's good, old-fashioned discipline might be just what I needed.

I dropped by the Triple-X Adult Bookstore on my way home from work again. In two weeks, I'd pretty well worn out the last copies I'd picked up of Twat Busters and Insatiable Brunettes. The Triple-X was nothing new to me. I'd been going there off and on for years. That, like spanking, was another family ritual. The day that each of us—Larry and Frank and me—had registered to vote, Dad took us to the Triple-X. He said he knew one way or another, we'd end up there on our own, and he didn't want us thinking it was perverted or something. He said any man has more spunk than he has real opportunities to spend, so using a magazine now and then to get off was perfectly natural.

Anyway, there I was, picking up a couple of new pussy anthologies. The Triple X was small—two aisles, one straight and one gay. As I came out and headed for the counter, I noticed a small publication on the rack between the two sections.

It was called "The Woodshed."

On the cover, there was a drawing of two guys. One of them had a big frown on his face, a paddle in his hand, and the other guy was being held firmly across his knee. That one had his pants down to his ankles and looked to be yelling his head off. There was a dark flush across his ass cheeks. It was pretty apparent his butt had been taking quite a licking.

It was impulsive. I snatched if off the rack and put it with the three girlie magazines I'd chosen. At the check-out, the guy didn't bat an eye.

When I took it out of the bag at home, my hands were shaking. Inside, there were stories, and photographs, and drawings, and advertisements, all of them from men who were interested in spanking. Some of them wanted to get it, and some of them were willing to give it out. I thought at first probably it was a gay magazine. I'd read some stuff in Time and Newsweek about sado-masochism between gay guys. But there were ads from all kinds of people, gay and straight, some of them looking for "erotic spankings," but more than a few that stressed "old-fashioned discipline!"

I sat there, and I thought: "Well, asshole. Put up or shut up. If you need a good spanking to get your ass in gear, this is your chance."

So I went to the computer and I typed up an ad:

Straight W/M, 26—good guy but lazy—need old-fashioned spanking to learn self-discipline. No sex, just some

95

real attitude adjustment. Grab a hairbrush and whale my bottom like my old man used to..."

I decided to use one of the forwarding boxes the magazine provided, and then, just for the hell of it, I got out the Polaroid, set the timer, dropped my drawers, bent over the arm of the sofa, and—Flash!—figured I'd send a picture, too. Might as well go whole hog, and besides, I thought I had a pretty good butt and that might get me some more responses. I put everything in an envelope, stuck a stamp on it, and hightailed it down to the mailbox on the corner to drop it in. With the kind of motivation problems I'd been having, if I waited till morning I'd probably never have sent it off!

A couple months passed. I noticed at the Triple-X the new edition of "The Woodshed" had hit the stands, and, sure enough, there my fanny was on the third to the last page in all its cheeky glory. Still, by that time, I figured it had all been a waste of money. Most of the ads were from guys in big cities. Hell, I figured, your rump's safe. No need to worry. I was half-relieved, I admit. But I was also disappointed.

So you can imagine I was surprised when, two weeks after that, I found an envelope from "The Woodshed" in my mail. Still, I thought, it's probably some guy from New York or something. But hell no! The reply had a local post office box for a return address. I tore it open. The letter, typed, read:

Dear Straight, White Male:

I saw your ad in "The Woodshed." I'll be brief. I've been dealing with punks like you all my life. I'm more than fifty years old, but I'm in good shape and, I tell you, I can swing one mean hairbrush.

If you're serious about this, name a date, a time, give me your address, and I'll be there. I warn you—I'll spank that bare bottom of yours till it sings! And I'll keep doing it till your self- discipline improves!

For now, call me—

96

The Blisterer

I couldn't believe it. I was going to get it! Suddenly, I felt a little weak in the knees, just like I had when I was a kid and my Dad would yell to me and my brothers, "Get back to the bedroom! I think it's about time you got your bottoms blistered!" And, too, just like usually happened back then, I not only knew I was going to get a spanking, but I knew I deserved it. Even at twenty-six.

I went directly to the dining room, pulled out a piece of note paper, and wrote back. My palms were sweaty and the pen was a little shaky in my hand, so I made it short and sweet:

Dear Blisterer:

I really appreciate your letter. I really need a good, hard spanking—pants down, over your knee, with the hairbrush.

I glanced over at the calendar. Okay, I thought, give him a little time—one week from today, Tuesday at seven o'clock. I put that and my address in the letter, and, once again, took it right to the mailbox.

What followed was a week of terrible anticipation. After all, it had been eight years since I'd gotten a spanking. That humdinger had left me in tears and my bottom red and sore for days. But I was still a teenager then, even if a pretty old one. Now, I was a grown man. Was I really asking for that kind of pain and humiliation again?

Every so often over those days, I'd walk into the dining room and see one of the chairs, and suddenly picture myself, bare butted, kicking and squirming over some older man's knee. Or, after a shower, I'd catch sight of my butt in the mirror—white, round, pretty hairy really. What would it look like after a sound dose of the hairbrush? Was I ready to deliver myself over to a guy who called himself "The Blisterer," for God's sake?

At the same time, there I'd be at night—kicked back, fly down, stroking away at my six and a half with one hand and sipping a scotch from the other while I watched some pussy flick on the VCR. Dishes need washing, I'd think. You could have a look at that Waller ford contract. You need to bone up on that new pc program. But I'd just lie there, pulling my pud.

"Goddamn," I'd say after I jacked away yet another evening, "Do you ever need to see The Blisterer bad!"

The big night arrived. I admit, I got home and immediately poured myself a double. I was shaky, and still not sure if I really wanted to go through with this. I wasn't in the house ten minutes before the doorbell rang.

"What the fuck! It's only six-thirty!" I growled.

I went to the door, opened it. And there was Dad.

"Howdy, Brett," he said jovially. "I was late getting out of the office and I had a couple things I wanted to show you anyhow, so I thought I'd drop by."

I was stunned. How was I going to explain that I had a seven o'clock appointment with a guy who was going to beat my butt just like he used to do?

"Can I come in?" he asked.

"Oh, sure, Dad, sure," I said, "It's just that...ahh, I've got to leave in just a few minutes."

I could walk him out, get in the car, drive around the block, and still be back in time to meet The Blisterer.

"Oh, this won't take long." He stepped inside. "Pour me a drink?"

"Oh, yeah. Yeah. Come on back."

We walked back to the dining room, and Dad sat down. He set his briefcase on the table. I brought him a Scotch, and freshened mine up while I was at it.

"Whew! You've got a pretty strong one going there," Dad said, eyeing my glass.

"Yeah, well. You know, lot's of work."

He nodded. "Say, how are things going with that consulting? Keeping on top of things?"

"Oh, yeah," I said vaguely.

He raised his eyebrows. "Sure hope so," he said.

"Ah, look, Dad." It was twenty of seven now. "Ah, I've really got to get going. Can this wait?"

"Oh, don't worry. This'll just take a second." He popped the latch on the briefcase. "I was just wondering if you'd seen this magazine..."

He reached inside, and then pulled something out, and threw it on the table.

"Oh, Jesus!" I whispered.

It was "The Woodshed".

Not only was it the magazine, but it was opened to my page, with my ad circled in red with, of course, my ass right there next to it, naked and spread over the arm of the couch.

"That's you, isn't it?" Dad said softly.

I slumped down in the chair next to him. How was I going to explain this?

"For God's sake, Brett..." he began.

I could just hear what was coming—"talk to the pastor," "talk to a shrink," "what's the matter with you?", "didn't we raise you right?"

"What do you think you're doing, flashing your fanny

99

around in some national magazine? Putting an ad in to get your bottom spanked!" Dad said grimly, "Didn't you ever think that I might go by the Triple-X? That I might glance at "The Woodshed?"

Of course, why hadn't it occurred to me? He was the one who took me there in the first place. Just out of curiosity, he might flip through almost anything.

"I mean, with the picture, it's pretty obvious. That's your sofa. And it hasn't been that long since I saw that bottom of yours, young man!"

"No." I mumbled, staring at the floor. What a prick I was, I thought. What a stupid stunt. What was I thinking? "Dad, I mean, just..."

"You just shut your mouth a minute!" His voice rose angrily. "Do you think, when you're having problems, you couldn't come to me? You stupid S.O.B.—no disrespect to your mother. You're damn right in that ad. You don't have the self-discipline you should. Don't you think I haven't noticed it? But if you needed that taken care of, you should have told me."

I sighed. "Dad, look, I'm really sorry..." I looked up at him.

He was there, staring right at me. Then, slowly, he reached back in his briefcase. I gasped. He pulled out that same hairbrush he had used on me eight years before.

"I'll tell you something, Brett," he said hoarsely, "You're not near as sorry as you're gonna be." With that, he pushed his chair away from the table. "I think you're right about your lack of self-discipline. And I also think you're right about the best way to solve that problem." He looked at me sternly, a look I remembered vividly from my boyhood. "So, young man, I think it's about time you got your bottom blistered!"

"What!" I said incredulously.

"You heard me! Stand up!"

I sort of staggered to my feet. "Look, Dad..."

He reached out and grabbed at my fly. I jumped back.

"Don't you think you can mess with me, Brett. Get over here! You're in for one hell of a spanking!"

This was crazy. And besides, in about five minutes, some other guy was coming over to do just what my Dad was threatening.

"Dad, look!" He grabbed at me again. "Look, I got this answer to my ad. This guy's supposed to be here in..."

"Ha!" Dad shook his head. "For God's sake, Brett, I should give you another spanking just for being such a stupid shit. Just who the hell do you think The Blisterer is?"

Suddenly, I caught on. Dad had seen the ad, recognized my ass, written the reply, and now he had come over to my house to spank me. I was in a kind of daze, standing there stupidly. Dad reached over and grabbed my belt.

"I told you to get over here!" he bellowed. "Let's get on with it!

Loosen those pants and crawl over my knee. Now!"

My old man had lost none of his quickness. As I stood there, he had my trousers undone in nothing flat, and then yanked me off balance and across his lap. He got his hand in under my waistband and—swoosh—tugged both my pants and shorts halfway down my thighs with one quick pull. I felt the cool air on my bare behind, and then Dad's other leg locking across the backs of my knees to really hold me in place.

"Dad!" I said desperately, suddenly realizing what was going to happen.

"I think..."

TWACK!

"Ow!"

"You should have done your thinking before!" TWACK! "Before you got yourself in this mess!" TWACK! "Twenty-six years old and I've still gotta spank you!" TWACK! "Well, I tell you, Brett!" TWACK! "If I've gotta spank you..." TWACK! "I'm gonna teach you a lesson today..." TWACK! "You'll never forget!" TWACK! TWACK! TWACK! TWACK!

"Yee-oww! Ooww!"

At first, I tried to keep my dignity, though really, how much dignity can a grown man have with his pants down and across his father's knee? I tried to stifle my complaints, and not wiggle my rear end too much. But, Lordy did that hairbrush sting! It had been eight years since my fanny had felt the bite of one, but it seemed like it hurt even more than I remembered.

TWACK! TWACK! TWACK! TWACK!

"OOWWW! Dad! OW!"

My dignity went down the toilet pretty quick. Dad was whacking my rump to the beat of the band. I started to squirm my fanny around, but to no avail. He had me held tight with his arm and leg, and it didn't seem there was any way to avoid the tail-frying face of that hairbrush. I started to whine.

"Dad! OWW! Dad! Stop! OWW! Enough! Enough! OOWWW!"

TWACK! TWACK!

"I'll..." TWACK! "tell you..." TWACK! "when you've had..." TWACK!

"enough..." TWACK! "young man!" Dad shouted. The hairbrush continued its merciless assault on my buns. The spanking seemed to concentrate especially on the crown of my cheeks and right where my butt met my thighs.

"Jesus," I thought, "I won't be able to sit down tomorrow!"

"Dad. OOWWW! No! OWWW! Please! OWWW-WOOW!"

TWACK! TWACK! TWACK!

"Am I getting through to you?" TWACK! "You lazy..." TWACK!

"little..." TWACK! "so-and-so!" TWACK! "Advertise for a man to spank you?" TWACK! "I'll show you who spanks you!" TWACK!

"OOOWWWW! OOUUCCCHHH! AHHHH!"

I don't know when it started, but all of a sudden, my legs were flutter kicking in the air like some five year olds, and my rump was bouncing and bucking there across Dad's knee as I pleaded with him to stop.

This spanking was even worse than the one he had given me at eighteen. My ass felt as if there was a hot iron pressed against it. My eyes began to tear up.

"NOOO! DDAAADD! PLEEAASE!"

TWACK! TWACK! TWACK!

"OOWWW! NOOOO!"

"Beg..." TWACK! "all you want!" TWACK! "But you're going to get spanked..." TWACK! TWACK! "Till I think..." TWACK! TWACK! TWACK! "I've paddled some sense into you!" TWACK! TWACK! TWACK! TWACK! TWACK!

Then it happened. Out of the blue. My butt hurt so much I just went out of control. I started to squall just like a little kid, squirming and kicking and crying my lungs out.

"OWWW! YEE-OWW! OWW-WWAAHHH! WAA-AAA-AAHHHH!"

My head jerked from side to side and my legs flailed fruitlessly in the air, my rear end doing a desperate dance there across my father's knee.

TWACK! TWACK! TWACK!

"OWW-OOO-WOOWW-WAH-HAH-HAH-WWAAHHH...!"

Twenty-six years old and getting spanked just like a little boy! And reacting just like one, too. I should have been absolutely humiliated, and thinking back on it, you can bet I was. But at that moment, I couldn't waste the energy. Everything inside me was concentrated on that incredible burning my backside was suffering.

Dad's lecturing continued as he shouted over my bawling and the rapid-fire cracks of that hairbrush: "Discipline!" TWACK! "That's what you need!" TWACK! TWACK! TWACK! "Right where you need it!" TWACK! TWACK! "On your bare bottom!" TWACK! TWACK! TWACK! "Over my knee!"

TWACK! TWACK!

"OOWWW! NNOOO! WWAAAAHHHH!"

I don't know how long that spanking went on. It seemed like forever.

I wiggled and squirmed and bucked. My legs circled wildly in the air. And, boy did I cry—hiccoughing and sputtering and sobbing. But Dad didn't let up. I guess he figured if a twenty-six year old had to have his bare bottom blistered, it sure as hell better be a man-sized blistering.

TWACK! TWACK! TWACK! TWACK!

"WAAAHHH-HHAAHH-AAAHHH! WWAAHH! WWAHHH!"

My bouncing rump was so sore I'm not even quite sure when the last crack landed. All of a sudden, I felt Dad pulling me up off his lap. He stood me in front of him with my pants and underpants around my ankles, still squalling like an eight year old. He held me by the wrist.

"Now! Listen up, Brett! If you don't have self-discipline, then I'll sure as hell give you discipline! I don't care if you are twenty-six. I want all those pussy magazines out of here

104

tonight. And you can pour that Scotch down the drain, too! And I'm not kidding. Until things improve, I'm going to have my eye on you, and if I catch you sneaking a drink or down at the Triple-X, I warn you, I'll blister your bottom right then and there!

Now, you get back to your room and think about things a while!"

I was still crying loudly. The fire in my fanny raged unabated, and, along with that, it was beginning to sink in what had happened to me. There I was, in my own dining room in the house that I owned, with my pants down and tears streaming down my face, having just gotten thoroughly and soundly spanked by my old man!

I waddled miserably out of the dining room and down the hall to my bedroom. I collapsed on the bed.

"YEE-OUCH!"

Jesus, I couldn't even sit down! The slightest pressure on my tender ass was agony! The only position that was at all comfortable was with my face to the mattress and my rear end raised in the air. There, I caught a glance of my behind in the mirror.

"Oh, God!"

There it was, spread wide, a panorama of my hairy, twenty-six year old butt—red as a cherry! And it was blistered. Literally. There on my cheeks were two spots where the skin was raised angrily, as if it had been singed. Anybody who caught sight of my fanny would know just exactly what had happened to it. It didn't look like a man's ass. It looked like a boy's thoroughly spanked bottom!

I sidled across the bed, reached over to the window, and switched on the air-conditioner to "high". Then, still sniffling, I shifted my sizzling fanny around so the frigid air blew directly onto my battered behind. It didn't put the flames out entirely by any means, but it made my ravaged rump feel a little better.

About fifteen minutes later, I heard the front door slam.

Later that evening, I went to the can and took out the sunburn spray to see if that would help coax the radiance out of my rear. My hiny was still red as fire and hot to the touch, swollen a little bit and throbbing.

After I'd sprayed my hiny good, I walked gingerly out to the dining room.

There, on the chair where Dad had sat while he spanked me, there was a note.

It read:

Brett:

I'm not going to say I'm sorry. Tonight you got what you needed, and what you deserved! I've had my eye on you for the last six months, worrying about the way your life was going. Believe me, there were lots of times I said to myself, I wish that boy was young enough to blister, because I'd sure do it to him.

When I saw your ad, it dawned on me that you were thinking the same thing. I don't blame you for needing a spanking. Hell, I think a lot of people do. I'd have probably avoided a lot of grief if my dad had kept after my bottom for a few more years. The thing I do blame you for is not coming to me about it. But thanks to "The Woodshed" and the Triple-X, I guess that's taken care of now.

From now on, when you feel like you could use a spanking, you know who to call on. It's nothing to be ashamed about. And, also, I'll warn you, I'm keeping tabs on you, and, from now on, if I think you need to get spanked, I plan to do it just like I did tonight. I'll see you next week— same time, same place—and we'll see how you're getting along.

- Your Dad, The Blisterer -

He did come by the next week and again left me in tears with a blazing bottom. The same was true the next week, and the week after that. In fact, for the next three months, I got a good spanking from my dad every Tuesday evening, until he decided I'd gotten my act together and picked up the self-discipline I needed.

That was eight years ago. My consulting firm really took off and it's been going great guns ever since. I tell everybody I owe it all to my dad, which I do, though I don't go into details on exactly how he helped me out.

I'm married now, and I've got two boys of my own, and, believe me, they know I'm just as much a believer in old-fashioned discipline as my old man. What they don't know is that, from time to time, their own dad still gets taken to the woodshed.

That's right. Over all these years, I've still fallen down now and then in the self-discipline department, and whenever that happens, Dad's been there to set things right. He'll give me a call and "invite" me down to his office after hours. I know what I'm in for, and as soon as I arrive, it's just like old times—out comes the hairbrush, down come my pants, over Dad's knee I go, and he blisters my bottom off. At thirty-four years old, it still ends the way it did when I was eighteen or twenty-six or thirty, with kicking, tears, and my bottom bright red.

A couple of months ago, Dad had a minor heart attack, and the doctor told him to ease up a little. I figured maybe that meant the end of my spankings. Sunday afternoon, though, the phone rang, and it was Dad, who said he'd heard I'd been sloughing off a little bit while he was convalescing, and suggested maybe we better have one of our little meetings at his office. As usual, I sweated plenty for the next forty-eight hours, but I knew he was right. I had been screwing off too much. Still, it made me a little irritable around the house. It's tough dealing with your wife and kids when you know that very soon you've got to report to your old man for a spanking!

Tuesday night, squirming a little in the car, I headed down to Dad's office. I must admit, I was a little worried, and not just about my ass. Even if I knew I'd never outgrown the need for a good licking, I didn't want Dad's sense of his obligations to send him to an early grave! Maybe I could talk him out of it.

I parked the car and headed upstairs. The place was deserted, but there was one light still on. Dad's light. I went inside, locking the front door behind me.

"Come on back, Brett." I heard Dad call.

He was sitting at his desk. There was chair placed right in front of it in the middle of his office, and, next to his telephone, there sat that damned hairbrush.

"Have a seat, Brett," he said. "Over there on the sofa."

I did.

"You know, Brett. The doctor told me I better avoid any strenuous exercise for a while, and, I'll have to admit, spanking somebody your age takes a lot of energy. More than that, I can't hang on forever..."

It made me a little sad, thinking about losing the old man, though it relieved me a little bit that, and finally, here in middle age, my fanny might finally be safe.

"So, anyhow, where you're concerned, I thought maybe we ought to start to think about making other arrangements."

"Well, Dad, maybe it's time..." I began.

"Just hold your horses!" he snapped. "Just because I'm getting on doesn't mean your discipline problems are over. Frank!"

To my surprise, through the door walked my oldest brother, Frank—forty years old and coach of the neighborhood high school rugby team. He sat down in the chair in front of Dad's desk.

"Since I'm out of commission right now, Brett, I thought your brother could do the honors for a while."

"What!"

Frank smirked, and patted his knee. "Get over here, Brett!" he barked menacingly. "I think it's about time you got your bottom blistered!"

But that's another story.

Spanked In My Hotel Room as told by: Timely Tony

Written by: Christopher Trevor and Ron Bossman

THWACK! was the sound of the leather paddle as it connected with his on display and upturned rear end.

"OWWWWWW! FUCK!" was the sound of his voice as he was paddled and paddled, looking down at the floor as he lay across the other man's knees.

It wasn't supposed to have been like this he thought, it was not supposed to have been like this at all...but unfortunately (what a riot, unfortunately for someone so lucky all the time) it was like this.

THWACK!

"OWWWWW!" he bellowed, knowing he would get no

mercy here...

His mind then wandered back to how this awful spectacle that he was starring in had begun, and to add insult to injury more than an hour ago at that...

"Yeah, yeah, no problem Mr. Bodner, no problem at all Sir," Timely Tony said into the phone as he paced around and around the suite of his luxury hotel room, clad in just a pair of sheer thick and thin black OTC nylon dress socks and a pair of gold colored silk executive's style boxer shorts. "I took care of that deal for the bank real sweetly. We are *now* the sole bankers for that new and up and coming Computer Corporation. This company will make Bill Fucking Gates shit in his expensive under shorts."

Timely Tony puffed heartily on a thick cigar and glanced over at the wooden structure where his tuxedo was hanging, him ready to climb into it for a night on the town with the lovely lady he'd met the day before...that is if his fucking senior vice president would finish up the conversation they were having and let him off the phone already. Timely Tony had just pulled his tuxedo style socks and silk underpants on when the call had come. And there was no way that he could rush a man like Mr. Bodner off the phone, no sir ree, no fucking way.

"The way I see it when that Computer Corporation is running smoothly the bank will be raking in bundles just from the interest on the loans we gave 'em when they start paying them back Mr. Bodner, trust your boy wonder Timely Tony on that SIR! HEH, HEH, they don't call me Lucky and Timely Tony for nothin' you know Mr. Bodner, SIR."

Timely Tony puffed his cigar some more and thought how he hated, he just hated kissing up to this asshole vice president of his. As Mr. Bodner ranted on the other end of the line Timely Tony flicked his cigar ashes into a crystal ashtray, set the cigar down for a moment and gave his semi erect cock in his silk boxers a quick squeeze. Just thinking of the lovely lady he'd met the day before made his cock hard as steel. When she had agreed to dinner and a show for the Friday night when

112

he would still be in town on business he nearly went ape-shit. And what a surprise he would have for her when the evening came to a romantic ending he thought as he looked at his open luggage and spied the round black leather paddle that lay across his belongings. Oh yes, Timely Tony loved spanking lovely ladies behinds till their ass was crimson and till they were crying, begging for him to stop. Every time a lovely lady cried it made Timely Tony's cock rock hard...and then he gave the lovely spanked lady the good stuff. He snickered softly as he looked at his round leather paddle.

"Oh no, Sir, Mr. Bodner, I wasn't laughing at you," Timely Tony said to his boss. "MY uh, my date, she uh, she'll be here soon and I just looked at my reflection in the mirror. I'm uh, standin' here in just my goddamned socks and underpants."

Tony clenched his teeth as he imagined his boss picturing him that way. Why the fuck did he have to have gone and told him that just then Timely Tony wondered and gripped the phone hard in his huge fist. But did his boss care and hang up and let him be on his way? NO! The fucking guy had to comment on how the lady was picking Timely Tony up in his hotel room...how he was not being the gentleman and meeting her at her place.

Timely Tony wondered how he could tell his boss, a vice president no less, that the lady he was meeting for tonight's romp was a married bitch and that she truly deserved the spanking she would be receiving at the evening's end? A married woman and it would seem mighty suspicious to be picking her up at her place. Hardy har and fucking har Timely Tony said to himself... Timely Tony wondered how many married women his vice president fooled around with from time to time. Being that Mr. Bodner was not married he could have his pick of many litters the burly executive thought with total jealousy.

"Yes, Mr. Bodner, I assure you Sir, everything went well at that meeting today," the broad-shouldered and hunky Timely Tony said, trying to sound reassuring to the vice president and wanting so badly to climb into his monkey suit and be on his way for a wonderful night out and then in when he spanked the pretty lady.

As he took a few more puffs on his cigar he heard a knock at his hotel room door. He quickly glanced at the digital clock on his night table, thinking that if that were his date she was about a half hour early in arriving. He also thought how if that was his date how she would find him looking real sexy and brawny in just his socks and sexy looking silk under shorts, hardy fucking har and har.

"Hold on Mr. Bodner, there's someone knocking at my door, SIR," Timely Tony said, lowered the phone from his ear and yelled out, "Yeah, who is it?"

"Room Service Sir," a male, young sounding voice responded from outside the hotel room.

"Shit," Timely Tony whispered and quickly placed the phone back to his ear. "Mr. Bodner, with your permission SIR, can we finish this later?"

Timely Tony smiled with relief as the VP said "of course" and wished him a lovely evening, adding that he would see him back at the office on Monday morning when he returned from his trip. Timely Tony hung up the phone and was about to grab his tuxedo pants when the bellboy knocked again.

"ALRIGHT, I'm comin' I'm comin' hold your goddamned water, huh?" Timely Tony called out and padded to the door in just his sheer thick and thin socks and silk gold colored boxer shorts.

He figured if the bellboy was alone it was no big fucking deal if he was not fully dressed. He was sure that like him the bellboy had been in countless locker rooms in his time. The burly executive opened the door and saw a blond, prettily handsome bellboy with piercing blue eyes standing there. In his hand was a large mesh-like bag of some sort.

"YEAH?" Timely Tony said in the handsome young man's face, his cigar smoldering in his craw.

"Your uh, towels, bars of soap and extra shampoos and body lotions that you requested Mister uh..." the bellboy said nervously, waving his hand from side to side to shield his face from the cigar smoke.

"YEAH, yeah, whatever, bring em' in, bring em' in, you know where they belong, or did they not teach you that in bellboy school?" Timely Tony said, grabbing the bellboy's arm and almost yanking him into the room.

"Uh, yes Sir, I mean, no Sir, there's no bellboy school," the bellboy said and walked slowly toward the bathroom as Timely Tony slammed the door to the suite closed.

"Jeez Blondie, I ordered that stuff sent up two hours ago, what'd you do take the scenic route?" Timely Tony said to the bellboy's back as he headed for the bathroom.

Timely Tony noticed the twenty something year old bellboy's tight ass in his black uniform trousers. It actually looked like two perfectly round coconuts that the kid had in his uniform trousers. The burly executive chewed his cigar, puffed it and thought how the kid's ass looked like a pretty ladies ass, oh hardy fucking har and har again.

The bellboy turned around and stared hard at Timely Tony...

"Two of the other bellboys called in sick Sir, we're short staffed today...and..." the bellboy tried to explain.

"Yeah, yeah, I bet two of the bellboys called in sick, probably two faggots getting their jollies," Timely Tony said rudely and puffed his cigar. "Put the stuff in the bathroom and hurry up about it. I need to get dressed and be on my fucking way. I got a date with a lovely, lovely tonight...not that you would know anything about something like that..."

The bellboy pursed his lips together in anger and stomped to Timely Tony's bathroom...

While the bellboy placed the items in the bathroom

115

Timely Tony took a few last puffs and then crushed out what was left of his cigar in the crystal ashtray.

"Fuck, I cannot believe that asshole Bodner kept me on the goddamned phone all that time and now I'm standing here in my stinking socks and sexy underpants while a prissy bellboy prances around in my hotel bathroom..." Timely Tony said loud enough for the bellboy to hear. "HEY! You almost done in there Blondie?"

"Just about Sir," the blond doe eyed bellboy called back. "Just uh, I'm just straightening a few things out in here for you Sir!"

"Well, if you're thinking that's gonna get you a hefty tip you can forget it Blondie!" Timely Tony snickered loudly. "Being that you were late in getting that sexy butt of yours up here cost you your tip!"

Once more the bellboy pursed his lips together in anger...

A few moments later the bellboy came out of the bathroom with the used towels that Timely Tony had left on the floor after having taken his shower.

"Seein' as you're here Blondie you can empty my ashtray and make up that bed and straighten out the couch cushions for me too," Timely Tony said meanly. "I needed a rest after all the business I had to attend to today in town, not that a prissy guy like you would know about that stuff either."

"I, uh, I'll make up the bed for you Sir, but I'm not a maid, that is actually their job you know and..." the bellboy said, glancing at the bed and then at Timely Tony's opened luggage, which was placed almost next to the bed.

"Yeah, yeah, yeah, and as Seinfeld would say yadda, yadda, yadda," Timely Tony said mockingly to the bellboy. "You're not a maid but I bet you'd look real pretty in a maid's uniform Blondie, and what the fuck are you lookin' at my luggage for huh? You think maybe if you organize my luggage

116

I'll reconsider giving you a tip or something?"

The bellboy could not believe the man's arrogance or his blatant homophobia. He had all too do to keep himself from telling this asshole in his socks and under shorts to go fuck himself and walk out of the room.

"N-no Sir," the bellboy said. "I'm just letting you know that I'm not a maid...and that I would not wear a maid's uniform..."

"NAW, you're not..." Timely Tony said, firing up another cigar and brazenly scratching his balls as he did so.

The bellboy could not help but note the sizable magnitude of the bulge in Timely Tony's sexy looking silk boxer shorts.

"And naw, you don't wear a maid's uniform, I just meant that a pretty blond boy like you would sure look real prissy in a maid's uniform, HARRRRRR!" Timely Tony laughed.

"That's unnecessary Sir," the bellboy said as he yanked the sheets down on Timely Tony's bed, noticing the pre cum stains on the sheets.

He grimaced a bit at the sight of the stains but stripped the bed nonetheless. It was as he glanced at the luggage a second time that his mind registered what it didn't earlier, the sight of the round leather paddle lying atop Timely Tony's clothing in the luggage.

Timely Tony again caught the bellboy looking at his luggage, and realized that this time the blond kid was taking in the sight of his round leather paddle. The burly scantily clad executive decided to have a little fun with him. He still had time before his date after all.

"You looking at something there Blondie?" Timely Tony asked the bellboy.

The bellboy turned red and angrier at the same time. He really was learning to hate this man.

117

"No Sir, nothing at all Sir," the bellboy quickly said.

"Oh, I think you had your eye on this," Timely Tony said, stepped over to the nervous bellboy, picked up the paddle from his luggage and held it up.

He thwacked his own hand with it a couple of times. The sound made the bellboy wince a couple of times.

"You ever use one of these on anybody Blondie?" Timely Tony asked the bellboy and thwacked his hand again, making the poor kid wince again.

The bellboy decided he had had enough of this and decided to play along. He felt his sadistic side coming to life.

"As a matter of fact, yes Sir, I have," the bellboy replied.

"Yeah, I bet your boyfriend uses one on you huh Blondie? HARRRRRRR!" Timely Tony laughed as he was having a great time taunting this girly boy. "I could see you squirming over some faggot's lap Blondie. I bet he spanks you with his finger jammed up your asshole too huh? HARRRRRRRR!"

The burly Timely Tony could tell that the bellboy was furious at this point.

"I uh, I better finish making up the bed Sir," the bellboy said and Timely Tony could tell that he had really gotten to the kid at this point.

At that moment an idea came to Timely Tony's twisted mind.

"So, are you trying to tell me you've used a paddle on someone else or, was it the other way around Blondie?" Timely Tony asked the bellboy. "Fess up here..."

The bellboy could tell that this executive was really pushing him now. He wondered how this scenario would wind up playing out.

118

"Yes, yes Sir, I have," the bellboy said, trying to sound as dumb as possible now. "I have spanked others with a leather paddle."

As the bellboy turned beet red with humiliation Timely Tony decided to call his bluff.

"I think you're lying," Timely Tony said, holding up the paddle. "Would you care to make a little wager? The winner gets to paddle the other guy's ass. If you are telling the truth and win you should easily know how to use this paddle. On the other hand if you lose Pretty Boy I get to paddle your ass. And believe me, the way I paddle you won't sit for a week or more. What do you say?"

The bellboy looked at Timely Tony with total fear showing in his beautiful blue eyes.

"Look, I have a deck of cards, we'll make it real fucking easy," Timely Tony said, puffing cigar smoke in the bellboy's face. "High card wins, okay?"

Timely Tony had won many times over in high card draws. He knew his luck would shine on him as it always did and he would get to paddle this guy's ass for sure and then he would head out for his date and then he would spank the lovely lady later that night. Oh what a night it had turned out to be the well-toned executive thought to himself...

The bellboy secretly loved the idea of getting to beat this loud-mouthed homophobes' ass real good. It was a chance he had to take.

"Okay Sir, you're on," the bellboy said and with a grin on his face Timely Tony went to get the deck of cards.

The bellboy, who's name was actually Dennis had worked in the posh and very fancy hotel for a little over two years at that point. In that time he had seen many handsome executives parading around their hotel rooms in their underpants and dress socks while conducting business on the phone; and all while he did his work of delivering what they had ordered, setting up things in their rooms, etc. Very rarely did any of them ever pay him any mind. To big time executives someone like Dennis was just about invisible. Of course they always gave him a tip after his work was done, but it was while he worked that executives in their hotel rooms did not take note of him. But to this hunky and nasty guy who he was told by the manager at the front desk whose name was Tony Romano he was very visible, very visible indeed. The miserable bastard was a total homophobe, called him "Blondie" as if referring to some pretty girl and yet he had caught the brute checking out his tight ass in his black uniform bellboy's trousers. And now, to really make it interesting the guy had challenged Dennis to a bet where the winner would get to spank the loser's ass. When Dennis had seen the leather paddle in Timely Tony's opened luggage he had to admit that his heart had skipped a beat. He had to wonder what a topnotch executive would be doing with such a device. But then the bellboy simply figured that if Tony was as straight as he made himself out to be there was no doubt he enjoyed kinky games and paddling pretty ladies' behinds. The way he was going on about spanking Dennis figured that this homophobe was real sadistic when it came to paddling... Dennis prayed that he would win the bet...just so he could teach this fucker a much needed lesson. Could he win this bet and get to paddle this overly muscular hunk of beef? That was the question now running through the beautifully handsome bellboy's mind. Standing there while Timely Tony got a deck of cards out of a drawer Dennis took in the breathtaking sight of the executive clad in just his sheer OTC black socks and a pair of gold colored silk boxer shorts, very sexy, very vulnerable looking somehow. The silk socks and silk underpants also spoke that this was an executive with big bucks. Timely Tony's ass globes were shaped like two melons in his silk under shorts. His shoulders were wide as a doorway. His arms were huge with muscles that looked like knotted rope. His hands were as big as hams, big enough to punch holes through walls with no doubt when they were fisted. His stomach was flat as a board, tight enough to bounce a quarter off he guessed. The bellboy took deep breaths as Timely Tony shuffled the deck of cards three times and then turned to him. As he walked back over to the terrified looking bellboy Timely Tony said, "You saw that I shuffled the cards three times, Blondie, no chance of me cheating or setting the deck in my favor."

"No Sir," Dennis said as Timely Tony held out the cards. "Okay, you go first Blondie," Timely Tony said. "Choose a card, any goddamned card, and may I say that it's going to be a fucking hoot to paddle that girly ass of yours…"

Once again Dennis seethed but a small part of him was resigned to his fate. He picked the topmost card.

"Not a very big gambler are you pretty boy?" Timely Tony asked as Dennis looked at his card, a ten of clubs.

Jeez the bellboy thought, this hunk of beef will beat that for sure. Timely Tony picked a card from the middle of the deck.

"Okay, we'll show each other our cards at the same time," Timely Tony said, not yet having looked at the card he had drawn.

When the two men held up their cards Timely Tony's jaw dropped in shock and the bellboy let out a whooping squeal of delight. Timely Tony's card was a nine of diamonds. Timely Tony was actually in more than shock. This had been a simple bet. Why had the fates suddenly abandoned him? He had never lost at a game of cards, never, EVER. Now he had lost at a simple draw of a card.

"Sir, I believe you lost," Dennis said, grinning from ear to ear.

The bellboy would finally be able to really give it to this homophobe and he planned on giving him a real good old-fashioned spanking.

"Now wait a minute here, not so fucking fast," Timely Tony said, feeling at a total loss.

He had never lost at a game of chance before. He really wasn't sure how to react at this point. Standing there in his under shorts and socks he suddenly felt very vulnerable. Meanwhile Dennis started to take control. As Timely Tony was still standing there with a look of disbelief on his ruggedly handsome face Dennis took the leather paddle in hand. The bellboy then grabbed the chair from behind the desk and placed it in the middle of the room. He sat down and just as Timely Tony had done he started thwacking the paddle against the palm of his hand, grinning from ear to ear.

"A bet is a bet is a bet Sir," Dennis said, almost sing songing.

Timely Tony knew that he could not get out of this. The kid was right, a bet was a bet and the executive was never one to go back on his word either, JEEZ! He prided himself on making guys stick to their bets, and now, he would HAVE TO stick to this one. If he did not comply and word somehow got out (although he seriously doubted that would happen, but fuck, one never knew these days, what with the internet being the information highway as it was...) his reputation as being "Timely" would be ruined. He walked over to Dennis and stood in front of him.

"Okay, okay Blondie, you won fair and fucking square," Timely Tony said miserably. "How do you want to do this?"

"You're going to lie over my lap," Dennis said, looking up at the hulk of a guy. "You've been acting like a bad boy. And all bad boys get spanked while lying over someone's lap."

Man, but this guy was built, rock solid Dennis thought lustfully. It was going to be his pleasure to spank this mountain of muscles...and then some. Timely Tony himself though was feeling very, very embarrassed.

"I can't believe this is happening," the muscular executive said angrily. "Come on; let's get this over with, huh?"

He got himself down over the bellboy's lap and his cock betrayed him by getting hard in his silk underpants. What was up with that shit? To add to his misery Timely Tony could feel the muscles in the bellboy's legs. He hadn't really noticed before but this kid was very well-built in a lanky way under his uniform. Somehow the burly executive knew that he was really in for it now. Dennis prepared himself to beat Timely Tony's sexy ass. For the first set of spankings the bellboy planned on letting the executive keep his sexy silk under shorts on.

THWACK came the sound of the first swat. It took Timely Tony unawares and he thought, "Damn, that was hard."

"HEY, take it easy there Blondie!" Timely Tony chuckled.

He realized shortly afterwards that it was not a very smart thing to do. Dennis became enraged at the way this guy kept calling him "Blondie."

"Blondie, eh?" Dennis seethed. "I'll give you Blondie! Blondie is a rock group and a comic strip, my name is Dennis!"

Suddenly, the spanking got much harder.

THWACK THWACK THWACK came the sounds of Timely Tony's ass being paddled three times in a row, followed aptly by the sounds of the burly executive grunting in a man's pain. Dennis was furious over Timely Tony's homophobic remarks and the way he had treated him. The bellboy would be sure that the silk socked and silk under-panted executive remembered this important meeting.

THWACK THWACK THWACK

Timely Tony, looking down at the floor as his head dangled next to Dennis's feet was really feeling this. His ass was being fried by a prissy bellboy, JEEZ! He was glad he at least had his boxer shorts on, but what Dennis said next made the big guy's heart sink like the Titanic.

"Okay big guy, stand up and remove those boxers," Dennis said, having dropped the "SIR."

His entire demeanor had changed at that point and Timely Tony noticed it, he noticed it well. The burly executive could see it in the bellboy's face as he rubbed the palms of his hands over the stinging in his ass cheeks, enjoying the feel of the silk against his skin back there. He could also see that this prissy faggot of a bellboy meant business.

"I said REMOVE YOUR UNDERWEAR, NOW!" Dennis shouted.

"T-take off my underwear?" Timely Tony asked. "Look Blondie, you won the bet, you're getting to spank a real studly guy here, so how about giving me a goddamned break and let me keep my damned under shorts on huh?"

What Timely Tony was really worried about, and Dennis could already see the evidence of it, was the fact that he was plumping up real thick and hard in his silk under shorts. Timely Tony could not believe it but when the pretty blond bellboy had started paddling his sexy ass he had laid more of a goddamned hard on. The topnotch and take no prisoners executive could not believe that his manhood was betraying him this way. Dennis saw it as the guy was somehow enjoying all this and in response to Timely Tony's request Dennis whacked the paddle hard against his open hand.

"Underwear off Mister," Dennis repeated. "Don't make me say it again. I want to redden that ass of yours with nothing to protect it."

Timely Tony gulped at the kid's outright audacity. He knew that he could easily swat this blond faggot like an insect and throw him out of his room, bodily. But if he did that he would appear to be the sort of guy who cheesed on the rules of a bet. Timely Tony knew in his deepest heart that had he won the bet he would now be listening to this faggot whimper, scream and sob as he paddled his smooth ass cheeks...but alas, that was not to be. Yes, Timely Tony faced the fact that had he won the bet he would now be reddening this kid's ass three different shades of crimson.

"Look, we need to get this over-with and quick, I got a hot lady coming here real soon to pick me up for a date tonight and..." Timely Tony said, trying to reason with the bellboy.

"Your date has been canceled, Mister," Dennis said and Timely Tony's jaw dropped. "I want you all to myself for spanking purposes tonight."

"You son of a fucking bitch," Timely Tony ranted, sneering at the bellboy as he stood there practically sweating in his sheer socks.

The executive could feel his cock pounding in his silk underpants in fear, anger and dreaded anticipation.

Dennis pointed at the phone and said, "Call the lady and tell her the date is off. I'm your date now, Mister."

Timely Tony clenched his huge hands into tight fists and padded on socked feet over to the phone on his night table. Looking at the bellboy as he sat there with the paddle in hand Timely Tony dialed Linda's number. His heart was racing and his cock was throbbing and hard in his silk briefs.

"Hello?" he heard Linda say as she picked up her phone.

"Hi uh, Linda, hey pretty lady, its Tony," Timely Tony said, grinning stupidly as if she could see him.

"Hi Tony, I'm almost ready," Linda replied.

"Yeah uh, that's what I'm calling about pretty lady, look, something's come up here, business wise, and I won't be able to keep our date tonight," Timely Tony said, trying to sound as convincing as possible.

If he had to tell her the truth, that he was handing himself over to a prissy faggot of a bellboy to be spanked he would just die of utter humiliation, so he prayed that she was accepting his story. As Timely Tony spoke to Linda, Dennis was making a quick call on his cell phone for two reasons. The first, to have his buddy Alex cover the rest of his bellboy shift for the night. The second, to have Alex bring a very mean surprise for Timely Tony to his room. The bellboy planned to not only redden the homophobe's ass...he planned to also open him up good and fucking wide. Thoughts of Timely Tony's stink hole caused Dennis's cock to jut up more in his uniform pants. As Dennis hung up his cell phone Timely Tony slammed down the hotel room phone.

"You fucking pretty guy man, how could you have won that goddamned bet?" Timely Tony barked as he shucked off his underpants down to his ankles and stepped out of them, his hard cock swinging forward, pledging allegiance to Dennis it seemed. "I'm Timely Tony...I never lose at anything..."

Ignoring the man's rant Dennis pointed to his lap.

"So, you prissy bellboy, you got me to take my goddamned under shorts off, you want me to take my socks off too?" Timely Tony asked as he slowly made his way over to the man who would be his spanker for the night.

"Nah, you can keep your socks on not so Timely Tony," Dennis snickered. "You look kind of cute in them somehow..."

"Jeez man, what a thing to tell a poor naked dude," Timely Tony said miserably and then lay down across the blond bellboy's knees, ready for his second round of ass paddling.

"Fucking fuck, bastard," Timely Tony bantered as he felt the bellboy squeeze his hard cock between his knees. "GAWD, got my cock trapped too huh? Go ahead you queer fuck, lookit that HOT ass of mine staring up at you, women love that ass, you fucking faggot, how lucky you are that its you that gets to spank it red tonight, JEEZ!"

THWACKKK THWACKKK THWACKKK THWACKKK!

"FUCKER, Gawd that hurts!" Timely Tony bellowed as the bellboy started really whaling into him now...

Dennis knew that this miserable stud was his for the night...and he planned to really, really work the guy's ass...

Dennis continued paddling Timely Tony's ass. The sound of the paddle connecting with the burly executive's sexy ass,

THWACKKK THWACKKK THWACKKK followed by Timely Tony's grunts and wails of pain was music to the bellboy's ears. Dennis had lost count at twenty. Timely Tony's ass was beet red already. His cock was also hard as a rock squeezed between Dennis's knees. Evidently, Dennis surmised, the fucking guy *was* somehow enjoying this.

"Hey stud man, you enjoying all this or what? You're practically dripping pre-cum there between my knees," Dennis laughed good and hard, squeezing his knees tighter around the guy's cock.

Timely Tony's faced turned a shade of red that almost matched his ass.

"Fuck you, asshole," Timely Tony seethed between clenched teeth. "Let's just get this over with."

Timely Tony was furious now but at the same goddamned time he had never been so excited in the crotch in his life. As the kid played squeeze and tease with his cock between his knees and as he paddled away at his ass Timely Tony wasn't really sure what the fuck was going on.

After a good while of paddling the guy's ass good and red, Dennis decided to take a chance.

"Ok stud man, up on your bed, face up," Dennis said, having acquired a firmness in his voice that wasn't there before.

"WHY?" Timely Tony ranted from his bent over position over the bellboy's lap. "What the fuck are you planning on doing to me now? What the fuck is this all about?"

The guy was trying to act as angry and as defiant as possible, but in all honestly something inside him was very aroused all over this madness. His ass was stinging mightily and he knew that this faggot was far from done with him.

"Okay man, well, DAMN, you did win the bet after all," Timely Tony said, getting up off Dennis's lap after the bellboy had released his cock from between his knees. "Okay, fine. How do you want me?"

"I just told you, face up on the bed, NOW!" Dennis demanded.

Timely Tony got on the bed and lay down on his back. He wasn't sure what the bellboy had planned but there was no denying his hard cock as it now pointed straight up at the ceiling. While Timely Tony lay on his bed Dennis went over to the executive's luggage.

"Ah, this will do," Dennis said and pulled out four of Timely Tony's silk neckties.

He stepped over to Timely Tony's right arm and pulled it roughly up to the bedpost.

"Hey, wait a goddamned minute here," Timely Tony ranted as the bellboy tied his wrist to the bedpost with one of his own neckties. "What do you think you're doing tying me the fuck up?"

Although he was very curious and his damned cock would not go down he did nothing to stop the faggot bellboy from tying him to his bed.

"Shut the fuck up," Dennis replied as he tied Timely Tony's wrist tightly to the bedpost with one of his neckties.

He quickly went to the other side of the bed and did the same thing with Timely Tony's other arm. The bellboy quickly noted that while he was tying Timely Tony's first wrist to the bedpost the burly and strong as an ox executive hadn't made a move to stop him with his other hand, which at that moment had still been free. The burly, well muscled and well hung executive was beginning to realize that this probably was not such a good idea after all.

"How does that feel Stud? Can you get loose?" Dennis laughed.

The bellboy had never known a guy to get free from one

of his knots. Watching then as Timely Tony struggled madly Dennis began to laugh harder.

"Okay, okay, hold on now Blondie," Timely Tony squabbled miserably. "I don't know what you got planned here you fucking faggot, but you've had your fun at this point. You better untie these goddamned knots. All this has gone far enough."

But Timely Tony's voice was not sounding all that convincing at all. His cock was even harder than it had been earlier and his tone at that point sounded more pleading than demanding. Dennis ignored the foul mouthed executive and simply grabbed another necktie.

"Hey man, what all are you doing with my expensive neckties huh?" Tony asked.

The blond bellboy grabbed one of Timely Tony's socked ankles and raised it up over his head.

"OOOHHHH HOLY SHIT man," Timely Tony ranted as Dennis secured his ankle to the same bedpost that his wrist was tethered to.

Then the bellboy quickly went for the high socked executive's other ankle. Timely Tony was now practically folded in half with his sexy ass in the air, a ready target for his own paddle at the hands of a hotel bellboy. Dennis looked at his prize and saw that he was now positioned perfectly, *just perfectly* for what he had planned.

"OH FUCK, FUCK, come on man, Dennis right?" Timely Tony pleaded desperately now. "Come on Dennis..."

But Timely Tony saw the fury in the bellboy's eyes as the guy grabbed the paddle and went for his upturned ass. Thirty swats later and Timely Tony was practically in tears. Then there came a knock at the door...

Timely Tony could not believe how his luck had turned so BAD that night in his hotel room. He had only been having some snide and mean fun with the remarks he had labeled the faggot bellboy with. And now, NOW, this blond pretty boy had tied him to his hotel bed and not just tied him mind you, but he was tied up in the most humiliating of positions. Gawd, Timely Tony thought, folded nearly in half with his damned ass "AND" his asshole on total display. His gaping stink hole was a prime target for anything that anyone wanted to shove into it. Timely Tony knew when the bellboy had grabbed some of his expensive neckties and told him to get on the bed face-up that he should have just listened to his instincts and thrown the blond fairy out of his room. The guy had his fun spanking Timely Tony but the rugged executive had to admit that his curiosity was more than peaked at what was coming next. Plus he had lost the bet so being a betting man he knew the rules that dictated that a gentleman must follow in these circumstances. But jeez, to have been spanked like a little kid over the bellboy's knees was one thing, to have said bellboy have teased his erect cock between his knees was another, but now, NOW, tied up on his bed like this, and wearing just his damned tuxedo socks and spread out like a cheap whore... GAWD! The executive thought that his situation couldn't get any worse...until after Dennis had given him thirty hard and unforgiving swats in his folded up position directly on his poor upturned ass. By then Timely Tony didn't feel so timely as he choked on his tears...and as he cried he heard the loud knocking at his hotel room door...

"Oh good, Alex is here," Dennis said and put the leather paddle down on Timely Tony's night table...temporarily.

"H-HEY, what the fucking fuck you fucker?" Timely Tony prattled, craning his head to watch as the bellboy sauntered to the door of his hotel room.

Jeez but the kid had a sexy ass in those tight fitting trousers Timely Tony thought. More and more he hated the fact that he had lost the bet and did not get to spank that pretty boy's ass.

"HEY! Who the hell is Alex?" Timely Tony bantered crazily, trying in vain to get himself untied. "OH FUCK!"

Dennis opened the door to Tony's hotel room and a second bellboy with dark curly hair and brown eyes stepped in quickly. Dennis closed the door instantly.

"Timely Tony, meet my buddy Alex," Dennis said as he and Alex stepped over to the bed and stood on either side of it.

"DAMN, lookit this stallion, all tied up and wearing just his sexy sheer tall socks," Alex laughed, placing a small luggage-like bag on the bed next to Timely Tony. "And fuck man, it looks like you really paddled his ass RED Dennis."

"So glad you approve Alex," Timely Tony grunted, feeling totally mortified now as the two bellboys talked about him and his red ass as if he wasn't even there.

"Do you mind if I take a few cracks at his ass?" Alex asked, picking up the leather paddle.

"Sure, go ahead," Dennis replied. "But give it to him real hard...that's how he likes it, and this high socked executive is very used to getting what he wants. Isn't that right Timely Tony?"

"NO, OH NO, oh GAWD, my poor ass..." Timely Tony gurgled and suddenly the stinging on his already red ass cheeks began yet again as Alex took his turn swatting the tied up guy with his own leather paddle. "OWWWWWWWWWW! Dennis, you sadistic faggot! I'll get you for this man! OWWWWWWWW!"

THWACKKK THWACKKK THWACKKK THWACKKK

"Oh man, five to ten swats with one of these leather paddles is enough to have the meanest of men sniveling, even a goddamned football player would be crying," Alex commented. "But don't you worry big man; we won't be all that stingy with you..."

As Alex paddled and swatted and spanked Timely Tony's upturned ass cheeks Dennis slid the luggage-like bag across the bed and opened it. He smiled sadistically when he saw

131

Alex's collection of dildos. When he held one up Timely Tony saw it and screamed louder as he was paddled relentlessly... he screamed in pain from what he knew the two guys would be doing to him in between reddening and tanning his sexy behind. Jeez, he thought, his ass had become the main course that night...

At this point in time Timely Tony wasn't feeling all that timely (or lucky) anymore. He had been reduced to a sniveling crybaby. After Dennis the bellboy's buddy Alex had delivered the luggage-like bag filled with various sized dildos the fucking guy had taken a crack at paddling and swatting Timely Tony's upturned ass. Alex was as sadistic a faggot as Dennis...maybe worse Timely Tony surmised as the guy whacked, whacked AND WHACKED his ass over and over with the leather paddle... and he counted each swat he administered to the tied up sheer socked executive, mocking the guy with each crack of the paddle. By the time Alex was done paddling him Timely Tony's ass cheeks were the color of a fire engine. He could actually feel them burning and twitching as he lay there tied to his bed with his own neckties in a goddamned folded up accordion-like position.

"WHAAAAAAA!" Timely Tony cried when Alex stopped paddling him at number sixty. "WHAT a fucked up night this turned out to be..."

"He was supposed to be going out on a date with a lovely lady tonight," Dennis said to Alex and took the paddle in hand.

The two bellboys snickered.

"Well, he might have a date but it's us who got him," Alex laughed.

"So what do you say Tony boy, another good forty swats or so before we get to the real fun?" Dennis asked his muscular prize.

"OH GAWD no, please Dennis, no more spanking me huh buddy?" Timely Tony pleaded, his ruggedly handsome

132

face drenched in tears at that point.

But even though the muscular hulk pleaded Dennis went to work once more paddling the executive's ass.

THWACKKK THWACKKK THWACKKK

And even though it was work, Dennis loved doing the work...

With each swat Timely Tony clenched his teeth, balled his tied up hands into tight meaty fists and screamed and cried like a little kid.

Finally, when Dennis stopped paddling him the two bellboys each chose a dildo from the luggage. Dennis's dildo was about nine inches of latex, pink and thick. Alex's was a tad shorter in length but made up for it in width and was ribbed on the sides. He could just imagine the big stud's reactions when he started sliding this baby in and out of his exposed bunghole. And it was just that bunghole that the two bellboys saw needed some moistening up before they started driving their dildo devices home...

"AAAWWWWWWWHHHHH, AWWWWWWW you fuckers, fucking mangy bastards..." Timely Tony was bantering a few moments later as the two bellboys lay across his bed, their faces at his upturned red, RED ass.

Dennis and Alex were taking turns spitting into Timely Tony's exposed rectal hole and then flicking their tongues around in it alternately, as deeply as possible.

"Fucking faggots, treating my stink hole like it was a goddamned pussy," Timely Tony murmured miserably, yet there was no denying that throughout this entire ordeal his cock had remained as hard as steel.

It felt awesome somehow as the two mangy faggot bellboys ate his hole with gusto, but the tied up executive was not about to tell them that. His big juicy and sweaty balls dangled between his upturned thighs...a real pretty picture the bellboy's thought meanly as they took turns rimming the guy like crazy. The sounds of slurping filled the room as the bellboys meanly chowed on Timely Tony's asshole as if it was the best tasting thing on God's green earth.

"Fuck, I should fart right in your goddamned faces," Timely Tony snickered as the two bellboys ate his ass-juice, him no longer crying now but his ass cheeks still stinging like the devil himself had reddened him back there.

Holding Timely Tony's ass cheeks like they were a pumpkin and with his mouth in his hole Dennis said, "You fart and we'll paddle you till you have no ass left..."

Timely Tony quickly realized that he was in position to be making threats.

"Okay, his ass is as wet as a duck's bottom, lets get started with these dildos," Alex said.

"NOOOOOOOO OH PLEASE you guys," Timely Tony panted loudly.

Dennis grabbed the nine inch dildo and placed the head of it at Timely Tony's hole.

"You ready for this Stud?" Dennis snickered.

"Please, no, I can't take that. Come on you guys. I have never had anything up my goddamned ass, PLEASE," Timely Tony was begging now.

Dennis and Alex looked at each other and just laughed. Dennis worked the head of his dildo into Timely Tony's hole. The executive's hole was tight that was for sure. It was not easy getting the device in. Timely Tony could most definitely feel it.

"YEEEOOWWWWW, FUCK, PULL IT OUT! PLEASE!" Timely Tony continued to plead and beg but it was no use.

The guy knew that because of the way he had treated the beautiful blond bellboy that his fate was now sealed...

With one mean push Dennis shoved the entire dildo into Timely Tony's ass. The burly guy was past screaming at this point.

"I can't take it; you're splitting me apart, you bastards, OH MY GOD. Please stop this." Timely Tony prattled madly, inwardly wishing that he had never agreed on this bet in the first place.

"Hey Dennis," Alex said, grabbing Timely Tony's cock from between the guy's upturned thighs. "Take a look at this."

Timely Tony's cock was rock hard and dribbling pre cum like crazy.

"I guess he's enjoying all this huh?" Alex laughed. "Lets pull the dildo out and shove it back in a couple of more times, hee, hee, hee."

Alex laughed an evil sounding laugh and Timely Tony's cock had definitely betrayed him. Somehow he continued to be as excited as he ever was. Dennis grabbed the base of the dildo and pulled it out of the executive's suffering asshole. He then placed the head of it against Timely Tony's hole and shoved it in again. The bellboy did that several times and Timely Tony's hole was being stretched to the very limits.

"PLEASE guys, I can't take this anymore!" Timely Tony ranted but his screams had turned to moans.

He was obviously enjoying this. Alex reached into the luggage-like bag and pulled out a bottle of lube. Unknown to Timely Tony this lube heated with friction. The poor executive's asshole was about to be turned on fire.

"Hey Dennis, give the guy a break, here, use some lube on that dildo," Alex laughed. Dennis saw the bottle and grabbed it from his buddy.

"Okay, sure thing," Dennis quipped and then looked at his tied up prize. "You're lucky Alex here is in a good mood Stud."

135

Timely Tony looked at the two bellboys who had literally become his captors and wondered just what the fuck was going on now. He couldn't really see the bottle of lube so he didn't know just what the hell he was in for. Dennis lubed up the dildo and shoved it back into and out of Timely Tony's ass, diddling the guy with it, it seemed. It didn't take long for Timely Tony to feel the fire.

"HEY guys, what the fuck?" Timely Tony gasped. "SHIT, my hole is on fire. YEOW! PLEASE STOP. PLEASE..."

Dennis and Alex were laughing hysterically. They meanly shoved the dildo all the way in and left it there.

"How does that feel Stud?" Dennis asked.

Timely Tony's ass was on fire inside and out now but his cock remained hard as steel...

"OHHHRRRR you fucking bastards," Timely Tony groaned in a mixture of pain and ecstasy as Dennis extracted the dildo from his hole.

It came out amidst squishing sounds and the burly tied up executive farted loud and smelly.

"OH jeez, what a fucked up thing to do to a poor guy..." Timely Tony grunted and struggled fruitlessly in the bondage.

The position that Dennis had tied the guy in had become beyond uncomfortable at that point. Timely Tony's arms and bent back legs felt numb and they were tingling madly. But then, his thoughts on his numb limbs were cut off as he felt yet another dildo being wedged slowly inside him. Timely Tony's gaping and heat lubed asshole was literally being stretched past its limits now...

"AARRRHHHHH...I should kill you two for this when I'm finally untied..." the big bruiser of an executive seethed. "We had a bet Dennis. We made a goddamned spanking bet. No one said any fucking thing about porking a poor guy's hole."

But then, as the dildo went in further Timely Tony's

cock pounded big and hard and beefy between his upturned legs and droplets of pre seed formed at the tip of it. The big exec had to wonder about that. What was up with that shit? Was there some secret, perhaps dormant part of him that was somehow enjoying all these kinky hi-jinx?

"Well, we did spank you Tony boy, and we will again, so we really did stick to the bet now didn't we?" Dennis teased his sheer socked captive. "But let me as you this you fucking homophobe. If I had lost that bet would you have spared my asshole?"

Timely Tony could only let out a scream in response to Dennis's question as Alex slid the monster-sized dildo deeper inside him, his ass walls again on fire because of the heated lube that had been applied earlier.

"I'm sure you would have made mince meat out of my asshole had you won that bet you slimy fuck," Dennis said and grabbed Timely Tony's throbber, holding it tight in his fist.

"Jeez, it feels like his cock is vibrating electronically. Keep fucking him with that dildo Alex while I jack this guy off..."

OH NO, NO, I don't want some fucking fag stroking and choking my cock," Timely Tony panted, sweating in the bondage now. "GAWD, what a fucked up turn of events..."

But Dennis ignored his captive and began slowly masturbating him...

"OOOOOOOOOOOO..." Time Tony swooned, sounding like a woman, making the two bellboys laugh meanly.

"You know what Dennis?" Alex asked as he slid the huge dildo home in Timely Tony's rectum. "If a guy shoots his load while he has something big wedged in his shit chute the pain he's feeling intensifies about a thousand percent."

The two bellboys laughed harder and Timely Tony simply whimpered as Dennis stroked his joint harder, the big executive's size of kiwis' balls crashing against his upturned thighs...

"Yeah, I know what you mean," Dennis replied. "For some reason a guy's hole becomes real sensitive feeling after he cums...and cums...and cums...

All this talk about his most private regions was making Timely Tony more and more furious...

A few good strokes later the burly executive was humiliated all the more as he felt himself about to shoot a load the likes of that he never had before in all his thirty something years...

Dennis did not give up. Timely Tony was getting closer and closer. The bellboy could feel the executive's balls about to explode their juices.

"You FUCKERS...UURRRRGHHHHHHH..." Timely Tony grunted and shot his load all over his chest and face.

He had never cum with such intensity. Dennis and Alex looked at each other and grinned. Dennis was the first to speak.

"Tell me Tony, are you enjoying all this? You like having a fat dildo shoved up your ass?" Dennis asked and he and Alex exploded in laughter.

"Just wait till I get untied," Timely Tony said through clenched teeth. "You've both had it. You'll both pay for this shit! I had considered sparing you both, seeing as this was all just because of a bet and in fun, but now that you made me cum I'm going to see to it you both get what the fuck is coming to you! No faggots should get a one up on a straight dude by making him shoot his load, JEEZ!"

Timely Tony was spent. The dildo still in his ass was driving him mad *and* his goddamned cock, dangling between his upturned thighs, was getting hard again.

"Alex, take a look at that, his cock is getting all stiff

138

again, he must really like this," Dennis quipped and pushed the dildo in even further as he said this.

Timely Tony screamed in a mixture of agony and ecstasy. Then, Dennis reached into the luggage-like bag of tricks and brought out a vibrating dildo. Alex yanked the dildo that was in Timely Tony's ass out quickly and with no hesitation. A huge sucking sound followed and Timely Tony farted loudly. Alex and Dennis both laughed, waving their hands in front of their faces in mock disgust.

"Come on guys, give a poor guy a break," Timely Tony was again pleading, his threatening attitude once again gone it would seem. "I've been bent in two like this for over an hour now."

"What do you think Alex? Should we change his position?" Dennis asked his buddy.

"Okay Dennis, lets try tying him spread eagle face-up," Alex replied. "But first let's get this vibrator in him."

"OH NO, NO..." Timely Tony panted.

The executive's hole was so well-lubed at this point that the vibrator slid right in. Actually, it looked to Dennis and Alex as if Timely Tony's asshole sucked the vibrator in greedily. This time Dennis tied the dildo shaped device in place by securing a harness around Timely Tony's waist. The vibrator was not going anywhere fast. Once the vibrator was in place Alex released Timely Tony's legs and retied them at his socked ankles at the end of the bed. The muscular executive was now tied spread eagle and face-up. Dennis reached between Timely Tony's spread legs and switched on the vibrator. A humming sound filled the air.

"OH GOD NO, you guys have to stop this, that fucking thing is going to kill me!" Timely Tony pleaded. "Gawd, it's buzzing like bees in my shit chute..."

Fearful, the executive's cock was again rock hard and dripping pre-cum. He could not believe it. Alex and Dennis

139

enjoyed watching the big man suffer. Then, Dennis looked at the clock by the bed.

"Hey man, its' almost midnight," Dennis said.

Alex knew that meant. The two bellboys both had to act fast. Alex went to Timely Tony's luggage and opened it up wide. He started gathering the executive's clothes and shoving them in the luggage.

"H-hey, what the fuck are you doing?" Timely Tony asked feeling puzzled.

Meanwhile Dennis was checking to make sure they had gotten all of Timely Tony's clothing and personal items, up to and including his bathroom supplies. They then placed the filled luggage by the door of the hotel room.

"HEY, GUYS, you can't fucking leave me like this, COME ON," Timely Tony screeched frantically. "FUCKING FUCKS, just wait till I get loose. I will have you both fired for this."

Timely Tony was struggling crazily against his own neckties but the knots were too tight. The vibrator in his ass was driving him wild, sending him soaring to new heights it seemed. Alex and Dennis stood at either side of the bed.

"Looks like he's ready to pop again," Dennis chuckled as he and Alex salivated over the sight of Timely Tony's erection as it pointed straight up at the ceiling, the guy's cock caked up with his dried up cum from his earlier blast.

"Yes Dennis, it sure does," Alex agreed and with that he grabbed the tied up executive's hard cock.

It didn't take long before Timely Tony exploded again all over his chest and the rest of his upper body.

"AAAAWWWWWWWW FUUUUUCCCCKKKKK," Timely Tony gurgled in agony and forced ecstasy, the buzzing vibrator in his hole now REALLY sending chills through him.

What a night it had turned out to be.

With that Alex and Dennis turned and grabbed the luggage. They left poor Timely Tony without a stitch of clothing, save for the sheer socks he was still wearing, tied to the bed and completely helpless...

"That went well and as planned, the boss will be very pleased," Dennis said and had a smug looking grin on his face.

Alex nodded in agreement. The two bellboys both made their through the hotel lobby and down to the parking garage with Timely Tony's luggage. They walked to the furthest end of the lot where a stretch limousine was waiting. The trunk popped open and they placed the luggage inside, closing it tight afterwards. The window at the passenger seat of the limousine was slowly lowered.

"Well boys, how did it go? Did you follow my instructions?" the man in the passenger seat asked.

Dennis was the first to reply.

"Yes Mr. Bodner, he really thought we were bellboys at the hotel," Dennis said. "He has no idea whatsoever that he was set up."

"We left him tied to the bed, he's resting now, as you instructed Sir," Alex added. "And we're sure he's ready for the next step."

"Good, good, very good job as always," Bodner said to the two young men. "Here's your payment that was promised you."

Mr. Bodner passed the two young men an envelope each. Each of the envelopes was filled with $100.00 bills. Alex and Dennis were counting their money as they walked away from the limousine. They agreed that this was the most fun they'd had in a long time but now it was back to the racetrack for them. They wondered what would become of the ruggedly handsome executive called "Timely Tony."

"Yes, he's ready, proceed with phase two, and I don't give a rats ass if you think it's too humiliating, just do it," Mr. Bodner said and slammed down the phone.

Tony, or Timely Tony, as he called himself Mr. Bodner thought, was getting too cocky for his own good. His boy wonder thought he was indestructible. Well, this should shake him down several levels. The vice president smiled as he thought what the rest of the night would bring "Timely Tony."

Timely Tony could not believe what a fucked up evening it had turned out to be for him. Also, the rugged bruiser of an executive could not believe how the fates had suddenly turned against him...SHIT! He had been utterly and completely humiliated. Not only had he lost the bet to that prissy bellboy Dennis and wound up with his ass cheeks as red as a fire engine, but his ass had been turned into a goddamned buffet. Dennis and his sadistic buddy Alex had actually eaten his goddamned stinking hole...and then to add insult to that humiliation they had wedged and stretched him open back there with dildos... GAWD!

As the still tied up executive opened his eyes he glanced over at the digital clock on his hotel room night table and saw that it was 7:30 AM. His jaw dropped as he could not believe he had actually slept a few hours...tied up and with a vibrating and buzzing dildo wedged in his hole at that. Looking down at himself Timely Tony saw that his cock was rock hard between his muscular thighs. He wiggled sexily on the bed and his erection twitched...a dollop of pre cum oozing from his piss hole and dripping slowly down his shaft as he breathed heavily. He could feel his balls churning in his sweaty sac. He wiggled his toes under his black sheer thick and thin socks and wondered why the fuck his cock had risen to the occasion throughout what he had been put through the night before. He was straight and it had been two guys that had worked him over...but JEEZ, that Dennis sure had an ass like a sexy woman's. Timely Tony grinned lecherously and swore that he would take his revenge on the blond fairy. At the moment though he had other, more pressing matters to attend to...namely getting himself untied, getting the goddamned dildo out of his shit chute and finding a way to get his clothes back so that he could get out of the hotel room. It was Saturday morning after all and he needed to be on his way home...

As he struggled to get untied and as his cock flopped around between his legs Timely Tony's eyes opened in terror when he saw the door to his room open and two women dressed as maids walked in. Timely Tony gulped hard but somehow they looked familiar to him. As the two maids came into his room, locking the door behind them Timely Tony squirmed miserably on the bed, still trying desperately to free himself from the bondage that the two bellboys had left him in the night before. The two pretty ladies slowly made their way over to the bed that the poor executive was bound to with his own expensive neckties. He was spread-eagled with his cock rigidly stiff and a humiliating of all, a vibrating dildo wedged deep into his anal canal. The sound of the dildo buzzing filled the air and thick dollops of pre seed oozed from the well-muscled executive's wide sexy piss slit. Taking in the sight of the two maids Timely Tony somehow felt that they looked familiar. "HOLY FUCK!" he thought when he realized that they were two women he had dated recently, dated and spanked. SHIT! He struggled madly now to get untied.

"Bitches..." he whispered.

"Well hello to you too Tony, or, as you so like to be called, Timely Tony," the blond maid said to him, taking up position on the right side of his bed, leaning down slightly, her massive sized tits just about visible as she leaned down. "Now tell us, how did you wind up in such a predicament? Of all things, tied to your bed in just your socks AND with a dildo wedged in that sexy, sexy ass of yours..."

"Samantha, this isn't funny, please, untie me, two goddamned bellboys left me like this, and it was supposed to be a game, JUST A GODDAMNED game!" Timely Tony panted, his hard cock swaying back and forth, thick, hard and beefy.

The two maids giggled at the sight of the dried up cum

all over Timely Tony's muscular body.

"A game Timely Tony?" the redheaded maid asked from the left side of the bed, her leaning down as well and showing off her massive cleavage, her maid uniform barely concealing her ample bosoms. "And with bellboys no less? Have you switched over to the other team?"

"NO, NO, it's not like that, they were faggots and...OH SHIT, fuck..." Timely Tony bantered, realizing that if his feet weren't tied that one of them would have been in his mouth right about then.

"Faggot bellboys, you have indeed switched to the other side Tony, you've been a bad, bad boy," the redheaded maid said in a teasing tone.

"Jennifer, look what I found," the blond maid said, holding up the executive's leather paddle.

"Why Samantha, that is the same paddle that Timely Tony here spanked me with when he and I went out on our date a few months ago," the redheaded maid said. "He said he wanted to make my little fanny as red as my hair...AND HE DID. The bastard..."

"Okay, okay, I know what you bitches are planning here, but trust me, I've been spanked to within an inch of my life here last night," Timely Tony pleaded. "Those two bellboys spanked me till my ass was all red and welted. You can fucking see for yourselves. And after that they fucking wedged dildos in my hole and they took my goddamned luggage with all my clothes in it. All I got to wear are the socks you see on my stinking feet! So please, untie me, I'll do anything you want!"

As Timely Tony pleaded Samantha leaned down further, took the executive's cock in her mouth and as she sucked his erection Jennifer tied a silk black blindfold over the bound up executive's eyes, her tits right in his face as she did so...

"OHHHHHH...fucking fuck...what do you two bitches have in mind for me?" Timely Tony grunted in a mixture of ecstasy and fear.

While Samantha was busy sucking Timely Tony's cock Jennifer went to work tying a rope around the bound up executive's huge balls. Timely Tony was undeniably in ecstasy. He knew the bitch was playing with his balls but he had no idea what she had in mind.

"Oh fuck, man, that feels good," Timely Tony said pleadingly. "Come on girls untie me and then we can have a really good time."

Samantha backed away from Timely Tony's cock. The two women knew they didn't have much time. Mr. Bodner had been very clear with his instructions. Timely Tony's balls were tied up nice and tight at that point...with a long stretch of rope hanging off for pulling on if and when needed.

"Okay you big stud you, Jennifer and I are going to untie your ankles and raise those sexy legs of yours," Samantha said, sounding real sexy. "We want to take turns getting our tongues up that ass of yours. You'll like that won't you Timely Tony?"

Samantha sounded like she was doing her best to convince him making the big guy very suspicious. He had never heard of women wanting to eat a poor tied up slob's asshole. That was more a faggot thing.

"What do you two have up your sleeves? Can't you give a guy a break and let me go?" Timely Tony pleaded. "FUCK, it seems like my asshole has become the toy of the moment. Come on, this is embarrassing enough."

But to the tied up executive it didn't look like this was going to be so easy, convincing these two dumb broads to untie him. The two women knew that they had to work fast for what Mr. Bodner wanted. Samantha started to untie Timely Tony's left foot. Jennifer had the rope that was tied to the guy's balls in her hand. As soon as his leg was freed Timely Tony started to thrash about. Jennifer yanked on the rope, pulling hard on poor Timely Tony's balls. The bound executive screamed out,

"YEOOOOWWWWW" and he immediately stopped struggling.

"Listen Stud, if you don't cooperate we're going to pull your balls off, you hear me?" Jennifer asked and Timely Tony could tell that she was not fooling around.

She had no compassion for him it seemed. After the way he had spanked her the time they had gone out he didn't wonder why either. Samantha lifted Timely Tony's leg above his head and tied it tightly at his socked ankle to the headboard, adding rope in addition to his necktie. She untied his other leg and then raised that one as well. Now both of Timely Tony's legs were tied above his head, his ass once again sticking up in the air.

"Good boy Tony, now don't you look so pretty with that dildo sticking out of your sexy ass?" Samantha asked and she and Jennifer laughed.

Timely Tony's face turned beet red in a mixture of anger and outright humiliation.

"Okay, okay, what have you two sluts got planned for me now?" Timely Tony grunted in his once again folded-up position.

He didn't want to admit it but he was scared. The two bitches were not about to let him go. Still blindfolded and in such a vulnerable position they could do anything they wanted to him. Jennifer got the rope that was tethered to the executive's balls and tied it off to the headboard above his head as well, she tied it nice and tight and taut...

"Bitches! Fucking sluts!" Timely Tony seethed, squirming miserably and as much as possible in the very humiliating position that the two so-called maids had folded him back into on his hotel room bed. "This is a shitty thing to do to a guy..." "Oh really Tony?" he heard Samantha ask as she was slowly pulling the dildo that was wedged in the burly guy's ass outwards. "What about the times you spanked me and Jennifer here? Wasn't that a shitty thing to do to some poor girls?"

"You bitches, you know you loved it when I..." Timely Tony gurgled but then memory flooded in and he cut himself off in mid sentence.

Timely Tony pursed his lips together and recalled where he had seen the two maids before. They were most definitely both women he had dated in the past. And yes, he had meanly fed his fetish with both of them by spanking the tar out of them, making their pretty white asses the color of a fire engine. He remembered how he had sadistically teased each of them while paddling them with his trusty leather paddle. He remembered how their cries of ecstasy eventually turned to cries of anguish. Oh and how those cries of anguish had only spurred him on all the more. And how hard in the cock it had made him to hear those pretty ladies crying... And now, embarrassments of embarrassments Timely Tony himself had his ass spanked to the very same hue that he had administered to his lovely dates...and by a prissy bellboy, a faggot and two women. Needless to say the well-muscled guy was beside himself with anger and humiliation. He clenched his teeth as Samantha gave the dildo a few turns as she slowly and methodically extracted it from his gaping asshole. When the device was finally out of his shit chute Timely Tony breathed a sigh of relief.

The two maids then took turns licking Timely Tony's ass crack, scratching his balls hard as they stuck out from between his upturned thighs and prodded his hole meanly with sharp fingernails...

"AAAAARRRRR FUCK, what is this shit? Licking my ass and torturing my goddamned family jewels of all things?" Timely Tony bantered and curled his toes back under his black tuxedo style socks.

"Keep carrying on like that and we'll paddle your ass again Timely Tony," Jennifer teased him and licked his balls.

"OKAY, OKAY, fucking bitches, goddamned fucked up bitches, go ahead, work my asshole, eat all my stinking ass chowder out of my hole, work it for me you cunts, but please,

147

just don't paddle me anymore..." Timely Tony pleaded. "The way that bellboy and his faggot buddy worked me over was un-fucking-believable! I don't think I could take it anymore if someone paddled me again..."

Timely Tony heard the two women chuckle meanly...

"WHAT? What's so fucking funny?" he swore. "Get a poor guy tied up to his bed and then you laugh at him? Okay, look, I'm sorry I called you bitches and cunts and sluts and whatnot. But please, please DO NOT paddle me anymore, GAWD!"

"Oh Tony, before you're out of here you are going to be paddled again, and you will not believe in a hundred years who it is that's going to have that honor..." Samantha said and then slid her very dexterous tongue into Timely Tony's spread asshole, treating it like it was a pussy...

Timely Tony could not imagine what the fuck he was in for and just who the hell they could possibly be talking about. He lay there half enjoying and half hating what the two women were doing to him...

His cock throbbed hard between his upturned legs...

The two women then licked his balls a few times each, really slathering their tongues over Timely Tony's tender parts. He grunted and squirmed in the bondage.

"OHHHHHH...fucking fucks...if Bodner could see his boy wonder now..." Timely Tony whispered and the two women giggled.

Finally, after teasing the bound and blindfolded executive for a total of two hours the two women climbed off the bed. Timely Tony looked around in the blindfolded darkness as his frustrated erection stuck out from between his upturned thighs.

"WH-what's goin' on here?" Timely Tony asked. "Why'd you two stop?"

"Its time for us to go Timely Tony," the executive heard

Samantha say as the women were untying his legs from above his head.

"Oh yeah? And what about poor me?" he asked and the two women replied by laughing.

"How quickly you forget Tony, that's not good where being an executive is concerned," Jennifer said and whisked his blindfold off.

A few moments later Timely Tony was tied to the headboard only by his wrists, his legs spread out in front of him.

"Look, you can't leave me like this, PLEASE!" Timely Tony begged. "It's not bad enough I'm tied to this goddamned bed but I have no clothes! Those two bellboys that worked me over took my luggage! They took all my clothes! All I got are the socks I'm wearing!"

"Hmm, poor guy," Jennifer said to Samantha.

Timely Tony decided to use a tactic that he knew would work...

"Money, I'll give you money, whatever you want, however much you want..." Timely Tony said desperately as Jennifer untied the rope around his balls. "They took my luggage but they didn't get my wallet! I always keep my wallet safely hidden when I'm staying in a hotel on business..."

After the rope around his balls was untied Timely Tony breathed a sigh of relief and said, "So how about it girls? How much to get you two to untie me and help me get some clothes so I can get out of here?"

Jennifer and Samantha looked at each other and grinned...

"You know, I think we do deserve something extra for this," Samantha said.

"I couldn't agree more," Jennifer said.

"Yeah, yeah, now you're talking," Timely Tony said hopefully.

But his heart sank again like the Titanic when the two women leaned down and started peeling his sheer socks off his feet.

"H-HEY, what are you doing?" Timely Tony roared.

"Well, the bellboys got all your clothes Tony, we'll take these socks of yours," Jennifer laughed.

"NO, NO, I'll give you money, I'm offering you money and you're takin' my goddamned stinking socks of all things? OH GAWD!" Timely Tony ranted and struggled like a madman as his feet were bared...and there went the last of his modesty he thought...

As he lay tied to his bed and gasping, trying to catch his breath he watched miserably and forlornly as the two maids walked out of his room, his socks dangling in Jennifer's hand.

"My husband wore socks like these when we got married," he heard Jennifer say as they left the room, closing the door behind them.

"OH GAWD, OH FUCK," the bound up executive seethed as tears of anger filled his eyes. "What the fuck, what the fucking fuck am I going to do?"

As Timely Tony swore like a marine he continued in vain trying to get untied...

He looked at the clock on his night table and saw that it was now nearly nine thirty AM. Those two bitches Samantha and Jennifer had sexually teased him for nearly two entire hours...

He wondered what the fuck they had meant about someone that he would not believe having the honor of paddling him. He squirmed on his still red ass and anger seared through him when he thought of Dennis the bellboy, his buddy Alex and those two bitches...all of them had turned the tables on "Timely" Tony, but it was Dennis who would pay the price, and pay it dearly Timely Tony thought. He was the one who started all this as it was...fucking prissy blond boy Dennis. Timely Tony's cock swayed long and hard between his legs...

As he lay there trying to come up with some way of getting untied the need to piss was setting in hard and heavy. He had been trapped on that bed since the night before and hadn't gone to the bathroom once in all that time. As he yanked and pulled at the neckties around his wrists binding him to the headboard he looked longingly over at the bathroom.

"Jeez, can't even have the smallest luxury of relieving myself," Timely Tony muttered.

But then, outside his hotel room door he heard a familiar deep-sounding voice saying, "Yes, this is the room, thank you. If you would just open the door for me I'd be most appreciative." Timely Tony's jaw dropped and his mouth drooped wide open as the door to his hotel room was opened and his boss, his vice president, his commander in chief, his goddamned superior was ushered in by yet another bellboy, although once M. Bodner was in the room the bellboy beat a hasty retreat.

"Mister, Mister Bodner, Sir," Timely Tony sputtered.

As M. Bodner sauntered over to the bed Timely Tony saw that the man was carrying a luggage, his luggage to be exact, the luggage that Dennis and Alex had taken with them when they had left earlier.

"H-how did you get here Sir?" Timely Tony asked the person in charge of him.

"I might just ask you the same thing my boy wonder," Mr. Bodner said, putting the luggage down next to Timely Tony's' bed and then taking in the sight of his naked and bound up underling. "Tell me Tony, how did an executive of your stature wind up in a state like that?"

Timely Tony gulped hard before saying, "It's a long story Sir..."

But when M. Bodner picked up the leather paddle from where Dennis and Alex had left it Timely Tony then realized what Jennifer and Samantha had meant when they said he was going to be paddled by someone very special...someone that he would not believe would paddle him...

"Tell me Tony, or should I say Timely Tony," M. Bodner snickered as he swung the paddle through the air a few times. "Timely Tony, I do like that, I like that a lot I must say. Now tell me, how many of our clients have you swindled in order to get them to sign papers? How many wives of our male clients have you had affairs with? How many of the ladies in the company have you spanked to the point where they can't sit for a day or so?"

"S-Sir, I did what I had to do for the good of the bank, you know that Mr. Bodner," Timely Tony gasped, spittle flying from between his lips he was talking so fast. "And as for those other things, well, I really have to say no comment Sir."

Timely Tony was enraged as his cock betrayed him yet again by stiffening between his legs and essentially pledging allegiance to his boss.

"No comment Timely Tony?" M. Bodner replied. "I'll give you no comment my boy wonder. Starting next week when you get back to the bank, and do not, DO NOT for a second think about resigning. You do that and I'll have you blackballed so fast your head will spin. You won't be able to find a job washing dishes let alone as a high socked and suited corporate executive. Now, as I was about to say, starting next week when you get back to the bank you will report to me twice a week after five PM, after all the staff has gone home. When you report to me you will be spanked by me for an hour's time. Is that clear Timely Tony?"

"Sir, you've got to be joking," Timely Tony replied, almost crying yet again.

"I said, IS THAT CLEAR?" M. Bodner roared.

"Y-yes Sir, it's clear, it's crystal clear Mr. Bodner Sir," Timely Tony said quickly.

"And if you fail to report to me for spanking I'll fire your red ass Timely Tony," M. Bodner added. "I have plenty of reasons that I could use to legally terminate you so don't even start thinking about lawsuits and all that suing the company and me crap..."

"N-no Sir, I-I'll be there Sir," Timely Tony whimpered.

Then, the bound up Timely Tony watched as M. Bodner shucked off his suit jacket and loosened his tie a bit.

"Now, what say I give you a preview of what you'll be enduring in my office twice a week from now on?" M. Bodner asked his underling as he approached the bed with Timely Tony's leather paddle in hand.

"Oh no, no, please Mr. Bodner," Timely Tony pleaded as his boss grabbed his ankles in one huge hand and with amazing strength lifted Timely Tony's legs straight up, the bottoms of his bare feet pointing straight up at the ceiling.

"OH GAWD please no Sir!" the executive grunted, his balls sticking out perilously between his upturned thighs. "I was paddled so much last night..."

"As I can see from this red ass of yours my boy wonder," M. Bodner laughed, rubbing the paddle against Timely Tony's exposed bottom. "And now you will be paddled so much this morning. Then I'll untie you so you can finally get dressed and be on your way..."

THWACKKK THWACKKK THWACKKK THWACKKK was the sound that once again filled Timely Tony's hotel room as his poor ass was again paddled...

As he clenched his teeth and endured the humiliation and pain he thought of what was to come once he was back at work and being paddled twice a week by this man. He also envisioned Dennis and the revenge he would reap on the sexy beautiful tight assed blond bellboy.

Discipline

About the Author

Christopher Trevor

Christopher Trevor was born in July 1963 and grew up in New York City. As soon as he was old enough to know how he began writing fiction and has been writing gay erotic/fetish stories for the past ten to twelve years at this point. He became an avid reader as well from the time he knew how and reads everything from fiction, to non-fiction to biographies of interesting and unusual people, people who have made a difference or who have paved the way for others. Christopher attributes his writing artistic inspiration to artists such as  Etienne, Tom of Finland, Tagame, The Hun, and most notably

Joe T, who Christopher has had the pleasure of speaking with and even meeting over the last few years. Christopher states, "Joe T encouraged me to write about my fetish because I was embarrassed about it at the time. Joe T said that when we are embarrassed about something that makes it even more enticing somehow." Christopher totally agreed and never stopped writing in this genre. Erotic writers who inspired Christopher Trevor were: Tom Shaw (author of "That Day at the Quarry), C.S. White (author of Big Sur), Larry Townsend (author of countless erotic novels), and Mason Powell (author of the classic story "The Brig.")

Christopher discovered that not only did he enjoy writing erotic tales but that after his first bondage experience he had a genuine flair for it. Writing to erotic oriented magazines about his first bondage experience truly opened the floodgates for Christopher where this style of writing is concerned. Christopher thanks the handsome and muscular "Greg" for that experience way back in time. Christopher took "Creative Writing" courses every semester during his high school years and while other friends of his stopped writing what they loved to write about as time went on Christopher never let a day go by when he didn't write something... "I feel that if I don't write every day I will die," Christopher has said many times over.

Foot fetish stories and all things related; spanking fetish, erotic shaving, muscle bondage, tickle torture, and hardcore stories are just a few of the areas of gay eroticism that Christopher enjoys writing about and inspiring in others as well. As one internet buddy said to Christopher where the black socks fetish is concerned, "Until I started talking with you I never gave a thought to my socks when I got dressed for work in the morning. Now when I pull my dress socks on every morning I get a chill up my spine."

Christopher is proud of the erotic effect he has on people...

Christopher Trevor is also the author of:

The Executive Guide to Foot Fetishism and Office Discipline
1-887895-36-1

Executive Ties That Bind
1-887895-37-X

Don't! Stop! That Tickles!
1-887895-31-0

The Taming of Dominick
1-887895-45-0

Timmy and The Hong Kong Tailor
1-887895-30-2

Love, Torture and Redemption
1-887895-32-9

Timmys Ticklish Trials
978-1-887895-74-3

The Gym Instructor
978-1-887895-44-6

Milked
978-1-887895-66-8

Erotic Street Blues
978-1-887895-97-2

The Abusive Wager
978-1-887895-04-0

Terry's Appointment and Other Tickling Stories
978-1-934625-08-8

The Military File
978-1-934625-21-7

Quirks
978-1-934625-24-8

Timmy and the Evil Dr. Vonvellicator
978-1-934625-42-2

Blackmail
978-1-934625-47-7

Tickled Kink
978-1-934625-49-1

Humiliation
978-1-934625-58-3

Look for them where you bought this book
or TheNazcaPlainsCorp.com